In Prison and Out

Hesba Stretton

Table of Contents

In Prison and Out..1
    Hesba Stretton..1
Chapter 1. TO BEG I AM ASHAMED..2
Chapter 2. A BOY'S SENTENCE..7
Chapter 3. THE WEDDING RING IN PAWN..12
Chapter 4. OLD EUCLID'S HOARD..18
Chapter 5. LESSONS IN PRISON..25
Chapter 6. NOT GOD'S WILL?...28
Chapter 7. BESS BEGINS BUSINESS...33
Chapter 8. THE PRISON CROP ON A YOUNG HEAD...................................38
Chapter 9. BROKEN-HEARTED...43
Chapter 10. BLACKETT'S THREATS...48
Chapter 11. AN UNWILLING THIEF..52
Chapter 12. VICTORIA'S COFFIN..58
Chapter 13. GLAD TIDINGS..63
Chapter 14. MRS. LINNETT'S LODGINGS...67
Chapter 15. AN HOUR TOO SOON...72
Chapter 16. TWICE IN GAOL...76
Chapter 17. MEETING AND PARTING..81
Chapter 18. A RED-LETTER DAY..85
Chapter 19. VICTORIA'S WEDDING...89
Chapter 20. BLACKETT'S REVENGE..93
Chapter 21. WHO IS TO BLAME?..100
Chapter 22. THROUGH GAOL TO THE GRAVE..105
Chapter 23. OUT OF THE PRISON-HOUSE...109

In Prison and Out

Hesba Stretton

Kessinger Publishing reprints thousands of hard-to-find books!

Visit us at http://www.kessinger.net

- Chapter 1. TO BEG I AM ASHAMED
- Chapter 2. A BOY'S SENTENCE
- Chapter 3. THE WEDDING RING IN PAWN
- Chapter 4. OLD EUCLID'S HOARD
- Chapter 5. LESSONS IN PRISON
- Chapter 6. NOT GOD'S WILL?
- Chapter 7. BESS BEGINS BUSINESS
- Chapter 8. THE PRISON CROP ON A YOUNG HEAD
- Chapter 9. BROKEN-HEARTED
- Chapter 10. BLACKETT'S THREATS
- Chapter 11. AN UNWILLING THIEF
- Chapter 12. VICTORIA'S COFFIN
- Chapter 13. GLAD TIDINGS
- Chapter 14. MRS. LINNETT'S LODGINGS
- Chapter 15. AN HOUR TOO SOON
- Chapter 16. TWICE IN GAOL
- Chapter 17. MEETING AND PARTING
- Chapter 18. A RED-LETTER DAY
- Chapter 19. VICTORIA'S WEDDING
- Chapter 20. BLACKETT'S REVENGE
- Chapter 21. WHO IS TO BLAME?
- Chapter 22. THROUGH GAOL TO THE GRAVE
- Chapter 23. OUT OF THE PRISON-HOUSE

In Prison and Out

Chapter 1. TO BEG I AM ASHAMED

The small back room, which was the home of a family, was not much larger than a prison cell, and in point of cleanliness, light, and ventilation, was far inferior to it. There was a fair-sized sash window, but more than half the panes were broken, and the place of the glass supplied by paper, or rags so worn as to be useless for any other purpose. Besides this, the next row of houses, in this thick knot of dwelling-places, was built so close as to shut out even a glimpse of the sky from the rooms on the ground-floor of a house four stories high. The whole street had been originally built for tenants of a better class, but from some reason or other it had fallen into the occupation of the poorest, and each room was considered sufficient accommodation for a separate family.

This small, dark, back room had been intended for a kitchen. Close against the window stood the dust-bin, into which was emptied all the waste of the house, when it was not cast out into the street.

Fortunately there was very little waste of food; for every scrap that could be eaten was greedily devoured, except in very extraordinarily good times. It was fortunate, for the dust-bin was seldom looked after, as the inmates of the crowded dwelling knew little and cared less for sanitary laws. Even the poor hard-working woman, who had been struggling for years to pay the rent of this dark unwholesome den as a home for herself and her children, hardly gave a thought to the tainted air they breathed whether the window was open or shut. She sighed now and then for better light, and the cool freshness of free air; but darkness and a sickly atmosphere seemed to be the natural lot of all about her, and she was not given to murmur. She had grown so weary with the long and monotonous battle of life that she had no longer energy enough to murmur. It was God's will, she said to herself, finding something like peace in the belief. There was a darker depth of misery to which she had not yet sunk—that of feeling there was no God at all.

Her husband had been dead for ten years; and she had had two little children to hamper all her efforts to lift herself and them out of their poverty. She had often failed to procure necessaries, and she had never been so successful as to be able to provide for more than their barest wants. They had all learned how to pinch hard, how to eat little enough, and how to wear the scantiest clothing. They were always trying to trick Nature, who never ceased to demand urgently more than they could give, but who consented to take less than her claim, though the landlord would not.

The children spent most of their waking hours in the street, for there was a small boiler in the kitchen, and the mother took in washing, with which every inch of the small room was crowded. When the weather was too bad for them to be in the streets, they lived on the common staircase or in the passages, hearing and seeing every form of evil, and a few forms of good also, swarming about them; growing up amongst them, as other children grow up amid the peaceful influences of well-ordered homes.

In the mother's mind there were still lingering dim memories of a very different childhood, and of better times before her marriage. Sometimes there came to her as there comes to all of us, sudden flashes of light out of the misty past; and she saw again her cottage home down in the country, and the village school she went to, and her first place as a young servant in the vicarage, where the clergyman's wife had taken care she should keep up her acquaintance with the collects and the catechism. Most of the collects and nearly all the catechism had faded away from her remembrance; but many a quiet Sunday afternoon she had talked to her children of the vicarage garden, where flowers grew all the year round, and of the village green, where boys and girls could play unmolested and unnoticed; and how she left home to come to London for high wages, and had never seen it again. Then she told them of the gay and grand doings there had been in the great houses where she had been in service, until she met with their father, and gave up all the grandeur and luxury for love of him. And then her voice would falter a little as she talked to them of his death, and of all her troubles following quickly one after another, till she was thankful to have even such a home as this.

The poor mother was ignorant, but her ignorance was light and knowledge compared with that of her children. They knew nothing and thought of nothing beyond what they saw and heard about them. David could read a little, but Bess not at all. The thick knot of streets was swarming with children, and it was not difficult to escape the notice of the school inspector on his occasional visits, especially as Bess was thirteen, and David nearly fourteen years of age. The boy had begun to earn a few pence in the streets as soon as he could sell matches; and he was now getting a precarious and uncertain living for himself by "hob-jobbing" as he called it. The Sunday afternoons and evenings, when their mother's work stood still for a few short hours, were their holidays. She had no longer a Sunday gown to wear, but she never failed to put on her wedding-ring, which on week-days was carefully laid aside whilst she was washing, lest it should get too much worn with her hard work. Bess and David felt that their mother was different from most other women in the street. She did not drink, or swear, or brawl; and all their little world knew she was honest. They were vaguely fond of her good character, and David was beginning to feel for her a protecting tenderness he could not have put into words.

For a long while neither of them knew that she was suffering from that fatal and painful disease of cancer, which had thrust its deep roots into her very life. When he did know it, David's heart burned within him to see her standing bravely at her washing-tub, enduring her agony as patiently as she could. At last she was compelled to seek help from the parish; and the relieving officer, after visiting her, recommended out-door relief. There was no doubt what the end must be, and not much uncertainty as to how soon the end must come. Four or five shillings a week would cost the parish less than taking the woman and her girl, even if the boy was left to care for himself, into the house, and provide for her the necessaries and comforts the medical officer would certainly pronounce indispensable. He advised a carefully reckoned dole of four and eightpence a week.

Mrs. Fell was more than satisfied. Separation from her children would have been more bitter than death itself; but now she would have Bess and David with her as long as she could keep death at bay. The four shillings and eightpence would pay her rent, and leave almost fourpence a day for other expenses! If she could only drag on through the winter, and keep a home for Bess and David, she would not murmur however hard her pain was. She could bear worse anguish than she had yet borne for their sakes.

But there was one enemy she had not thought of. The wasting caused by her malady produced a craving hunger, worse to endure, if possible, than the malady itself. It was no longer possible to cheat herself, as she had been used to do in former years, with putting off her hunger until it changed into a dull faintness. The gnawing pain showed itself too plainly in the desperate clenching of her teeth, and the wistful craving of her sunken eyes. Threepence and three farthings a day—one penny and one farthing a piece—could do little towards maintaining a truce with this deadly foe, who must surely conquer her before the winter could be ended.

"It's just as if a wolf was gnawin' me," she said to David, one evening when he came in with a loaf of bread, and a slice of cooked fish from a stall in the street; "not as ever I see

In Prison and Out

a wolf, save once when father was alive, and you was a baby, and we all went to the Zoological Gardens for a holiday. It feels as if all the hunger I ever had had hidden itself away somewhere, and heaped itself up, and is all let loose on me now. You children, take your share first, for fear I'd eat it all, and not leave enough for you."

"It's all for you and Bess, mother," he answered; "I ate my supper at the stall."

He did not say that he had made his supper of a crust of mouldy bread he had found lying in the street, and was still as hungry as a growing lad generally is. Like his mother he was quite used to disregard the urgent claims of his appetite. But he sat down at the end of her ironing–board, and watched her by the feeble light of the candle, as she greedily devoured the food he had brought. It seemed as if his eyes were opened to see her more clearly than he had ever done before, and her face was indelibly impressed upon his memory. For the first time, as it appeared to him, he noticed her thin sunken cheeks, her scanty hair turning grey, her eager bright eyes, and the suffering that filled her whole face. The tears dimmed his sight for an instant, and a slight shiver ran through him, as he gazed intently on her.

"Mother," he said, "I only took fourpence all day for running two errands, for all I've been on the look–out sharp. Mother, I must take to beggin'".

"No, no!" she answered, looking up for a moment from the food she was so eagerly eating.

"I must," he went on; "there's lots o' money to be got that way. They all says so. I couldn't make myself look hungrier than I am; and I'll tell the truth, as you're dyin' of a cancer, ay! and dyin' of hunger. I know there'd be folks as would help us. I hate the thought of it as much as you; but it's better me than Bess. Little Bess 'ud be frightened," he added, looking at his ragged sister, for whose sake he had fought many a battle, and borne many a beating in the streets.

"I never thought it 'ud come to beggin'," said his mother in a sorrowful, faltering voice.

"Nor me," continued David, "but there's hardly no work for such as me, as don't know nothink. I'd have chose to be a carpenter, like father; but there's no chance of that. Don't you cry, mother; you've done your best for us, and it's my turn to do my best for you. And

In Prison and Out

beggin's the best as I can do."

David felt it a bitter pass to come to. Untaught and ignorant as he was, he had his own dream of ambition to be a carpenter, and earn wages like his father. He had gone now and then to a nightschool, and learned after a fashion to read and write a little; but there was no school where a ragged boy like him could learn any kind of handicraft, by which he could earn a livelihood. If there had been such a place, how gladly would he have gone to it, and how heartily would he have set himself to work! There was no one to blame perhaps; but still he felt it to be a hard and bitter lot to turn out as a beggar.

"I'll do it," he said, after a long silence, "not just round here, you know, mother; but out in the country, where folks ain't all in such a hurry. I'll take care of the police; and I'll be back again afore Sunday, and you've got Bess with you, so as you won't be lonesome. If I've luck I'll try again next week. There's kind rich folk as 'ud do some–think for you, if they only knew; and I'll go and find 'em out. Don't you take on and fret, mother. It ain't thievin', you know."

"I'll think about it in the night, Davy," she answered sadly.

In the painful, wakeful hours of the night, the poor mother thought of her boy tramping the roads in his ragged clothing, and with his almost bare feet, and stopping the passers–by to ask for alms. It had been the aim of her long–laborious life to save herself and her children from beggary. Oh! if this cruel malady had only spared her another two or three years, until David had been more of a man, and Bess a grown–up girl! She could have lain down to die thankfully then, though now she had a terrible dread of dying. But as far as she could see there was nothing else to be done than to let David try his luck. There were good rich folks, as he said, if he could only find them. She must let him go and search for them.

"You may go," she said, in the morning, after they had eaten together the few fragments her hunger had been able to spare the night before, "and God bless you, Davy! Don't you never do nothink save beg. That's bad enough, but remember both of yer, what I always said, 'Keep thy hands from pickin' and stealin''. Them's good words to go by. And, Davy, come back as soon as you can, for I'll be hungrier for a sight of you than I am for victuals. Always tell out your tale quiet and true, as your mother's dying of cancer and famishin' with hunger; and if they answer 'No,' or shakes their heads, turn away at once, and try somebody else. Don't stop folks as are in a hurry. Kiss me afore you go, Davy."

It seemed a solemn thing to do; he felt half choked, and could not speak a word as he bent down to kiss her tenderly. He put his arm round his sister's neck, and kissed her too; and then, catching up his threadbare cap, he went to the door, trying to whistle a cheery street tune. He paused in the doorway, and looked back on them.

"Good–bye, mother," he cried; "don't you fret after me."

Chapter 2. A BOY'S SENTENCE

David was in no haste to enter upon his new calling. He walked on until he had left the busier streets far behind him, and had come upon the open and quieter roads in the suburbs. Here and there trees were growing on the inner side of garden walls, and stretched out their leafy branches, tinted with autumn colours, over the side paths along which he pursued his unfamiliar way. The passers–by were more leisurely than those in the city, and occasionally gave him a glance, as if they both saw and noticed him; such a glance as he never met amidst the crowds who jostled one another in the thoroughfares he was accustomed to. This observation made him feel shy, and more averse than ever to begin his unwelcome task. It was past noonday before he could bring himself to stop a kindly looking lady who had looked pleasantly on him, and to beg from her help for his mother.

His first appeal was successful, and gave him fresh courage to try again. The kind–hearted woman had helped him to take his first step downwards. He met with rebuffs, and felt downcast and ashamed, but he also met with persons who gave him money to get rid of his pinched face, and others who believed his story, though he was several miles from home, and bestowed upon him a penny or two, feeling they had done all they were called upon to do for a perishing fellow–creature. Not one took any steps to verify his story, but passed on, and soon forgot the ragged lad, or remembered him with a pleasant glow of satisfaction in having discharged a Christian duty.

By the time night fell David was ten miles from home, and felt footsore and weary, for his worn–out shoes, bought at some rag–mart, chafed his feet, and did not even keep out the dust of the dry roads. But he had taken three shillings and eight–pence; and he counted the coppers from one hand to another with untold joyfulness. So much money he had never possessed at one time in his whole life; and when he lay down to rest in a lodging-house in a back street of the town he had reached by nightfall he could not sleep soundly, partly from delight, and partly from the fear of being robbed. If he had luck like this he would go home rich on Saturday night. Early in the morning he started off again to pursue his new calling, which was quickly losing its sense of degradation. If begging was so profitable a business, and he had no chance of being trained for any other by which he could earn honest wages, it was no wonder that the boy should choose beggary rather than starvation. David began to feel that there was less chance of dying of cold or hunger.

It was a pleasant autumn day, and numbers of people were about the roads, sauntering leisurely in the warm and bright sunshine. Again many of them were willing enough to give a penny to the half-shy boy, who asked in a quiet tone for alms. He had not fallen into any professional whine as yet, and he was easily repulsed, so easily that some, who refused at first to give, called after him to come back. There was a touching air of misery about his thin, overgrown frame and pinched face, which appealed silently for help. He was willing, he said, to clean boots, or clean steps, or do any other job that could be found for him as a labour test; but very few persons took the trouble to find him work to do. It was much easier to take a penny out of the purse, drop it into his hand and pass on, with a feeling of satisfaction of at once getting rid of a painful object and of appeasing the conscience, which seemed about to demand that some remedy should be found for abject poverty like his. Possibly it did not occur to any of these well-meaning and charitable persons that they were aiding and encouraging the poor lad to break one of the laws of the country.

Whilst it was still clay, though the sun was sinking in the sky, David sat down under a hedge to count over his heavy load of pence, which threatened to be too weighty for his ragged pockets. He had now five shillings' worth of copper, and he did not know where to exchange them for silver. He placed his old cap between his feet, and dropped in the coins one after another, handling them with an almost wild delight. How rich he would be to go home to his mother, if he had equal luck on his way back! Five shillings for two days' begging! Now he had found out how easy and profitable it was, and how little risk attended it, if you only kept out of sight of the police, his mother and Bess should never know want again. He felt very joyous, and his joy found vent in clear shrill whistling of the tunes he had learned from street-organs. He was whistling through the merriest one

In Prison and Out

he knew, when a hand was laid heavily on his shoulder, and looking up he saw the familiar uniform of a policeman.

"You're in fine spirits, my lad," he said, "what's this you're crowing over, eh? Where did you get all those coppers in your cap? How did you come by them, eh?"

David could not speak, though he tried to seize and hide away his gains; but in vain. The policeman picked up his cap and weighed it in his hand.

"You've been begging on the roads," he said, in a matter-of-course manner; "and you've broke the laws. You see yonder big white house there, over the garden wall?"

"Yes," stammered David.

"You begged of the old gent as lives there," continued the policeman; "and he says it's a nuisance, and must be put down. So you must come along with me."

For a minute David neither moved nor spoke. This sudden reversal of all his gladness and prospects paralysed him. He had known all the while that any policeman had the power to take him up for begging, and lock him for the night in a police-cell, and charge him with his offence before a magistrate. Not a few of his acquaintances had been in jail, and they mostly said it was for begging. But the thought of his mother fretting and longing for him at home, and the grief and terror she would feel if he did not get back on Saturday night as he had promised, flashed across him. The policeman was busy counting over the heap of coppers, and David saw his chance and seized it. He sprang to his feet, and fled away with as fast steps as if he had been fleeing for his life.

But it was of no avail to try to escape from the strong and swift policeman, who instantly pursued him. David was weak and tired, and could not have run far, if it had been for his life. He felt himself caught firmly by the collar, and shaken, whilst two or three passers-by stood still, witnessing his capture.

"You young simpleton!" said the policeman; "you're only making it all the worse for yourself. Why don't you get honest work to do?"

In Prison and Out

"Ay, it is a shame!" said one of the spectators; "a big lad of his age, that ought to be at honest work, earning his own bread."

"Nobody's ever taught me how to work!" sobbed David, standing bewildered and ashamed, the centre of a gathering crowd.

"We'll teach you that *in gaol,* my fine fellow," said the policeman, marching him off, followed by a train of rough lads, which grew larger and noisier until they reached the police-station and David was led in out of their sight.

It was a dreary night for David. In his anxiety to save all he could to carry home with him, he had not tasted a morsel since morning, and his meal then had been nothing but a pennyworth of bread, which he had taken reluctantly from his treasure. He had been thinking of buying his supper, and what it would cost, when his gains had been seized from him, and handed over to the custody of the police superintendent. He was weary, too, footsore and worn out with his long tramp. But neither his hunger nor fatigue pressed upon him with most bitterness. He crouched down in a corner of the cell, and thought of his mother and Bess looking out for him all Saturday, and waiting and watching, and listening for him to open the door, and never seeing him at all! His mother had said she would be hungrier for a sight of him than for bread! Would they send him to gaol for begging? Boys had been sent there for three days or a week, and his mother would be fretting all that time. He would lose his money, too, and go home as penniless as he left it. He hid his face in his hands, and wept bitterly till his tears were exhausted, and a raging headache followed. At times he slumbered a little, sobbing heavily in his short and troubled sleep. When he woke he felt the pangs of hunger sharper than usual, for he had been nearly a night and a day without tasting food, and his hunger made him think again of his mother. Hungry, weary, and bewildered, with an aching head and a heart full of care and bitterness, David passed through the long and weary hours of the night.

When food was provided for him the next day he could not eat it. He felt sick with dread of the moment when he should be taken before the magistrate. He saw other prisoners summoned and led away to receive their doom; but his turn seemed long in coming. At last it came. He obeyed the call of his name, and found himself, dizzy-headed and sick at heart, standing in a large room, with a policeman beside him. An old gentleman from whom he had asked help the day before brought the charge against him, and added to it that the boy had been in the habit of begging along the roads. There was a singing in

In Prison and Out

David's ears, through which he listened to the charge made against him, and to the policeman in the witness-box giving his evidence.

"Have you anything to say for yourself? asked a voice in front of him; and David raised his dim eyes to the face of the magistrate, but did not answer, though his lips moved a little.

"Did you hear the charge?" asked the magistrate again.

"Yes," answered David, with a violent effort; "but I were only beggin', sir; I never stole a farthing in my life."

"Is there any previous charge against this boy?" inquired the magistrate.

A second policeman stepped into the witness-box, and David turned his dazed eyes upon him. He had never seen him before.

"I have a previous charge of stealing iron against the prisoner—"

"It's not true!" cried out David, in a voice shrill with terror. "I never was a thief. Somebody ask my mother."

"Silence!" said the officer who had him in charge, with a sharp grip of his arm. "You must not interrupt the Court."

"He was convicted of theft before your worship six months ago," pursued the policeman in the box, taking no notice of David's interruption. "He went then by the name of John Fell, and was sentenced to twenty-one days."

"Have you anything more to say?" asked the magistrate, looking again at David.

"It wasn't me!" he answered vehemently, "he's mistook me for some other boy. I never stole nothing, and I never begged afore. You ask my mother. Oh, what will become of my mother and little Bess?"

In Prison and Out

"You should have thought of your mother before you broke the laws of your country," said the magistrate. "This neighbourhood is infested with beggars, and we must put a stop to the nuisance. I shall send you to gaol for three calendar months, when you will be taught a trade by which you may earn an honest livelihood."

David was hustled away and another case called. His had occupied scarcely four minutes. The day was a busy one, as there had been a large fair held in the district, and there was no more time to be spent upon a boy clearly guilty of begging, and who had been convicted of theft. No one doubted for a moment this latter statement, or thought it in the least necessary to inquire if the boy's vehement denial had any truth in it. Another prisoner stood at the bar, and David Fell was at once forgotten.

It seemed to David as if he had been suddenly struck deaf; no other sound reached his brain after he heard the words, "To gaol for three months." Three months in gaol! Not to see his mother for three months! Perhaps never to see her again, for who could tell that she would live for three months? It was only a few minutes since he heard his name called out before he was hurried into Court; but it might have been many years.

He felt as if his mother might have been dead long ago; as if it was very long ago since he left home, with her voice sounding in his ears. He seemed to hear her saying "God bless you, David!" and the magistrate's voice directly following it, "I shall send you to gaol for three months." His bewildered brain kept repeating, "God bless you Davy! I shall send you to gaol for three months." It was as if some one was mocking him with these words.

Chapter 3. THE WEDDING RING IN PAWN

No doubt it was somebody's duty to inform Mrs. Fell of David's conviction and his sentence to three months' imprisonment, but whether the official notice was sent to the mother of the boy who had been previously convicted of theft, or failed to reach David's mother through the post, we do not know. She never received the information.

Mrs. Fell and Bess felt the time pass heavily while he was away. The poor woman had always been more careful of her children than the neighbours were; and she had never allowed Bess to play about the streets, if David was not at hand to take care of her. Bess was growing a tall and pretty girl now, and needed more than ever to have somebody to

In Prison and Out

look after her. So she was compelled to stay indoors, shut up in the close and tainted atmosphere, and the dim light of their miserable home. Mrs. Fell did a little washing still by stealth, but she was fearful of the relieving officer finding her at her tub, and taking off her allowance. She could earn only a few pence, and that with sharp pain; but the pangs of hunger were sharper. Bess was old enough and willing to help, though she could not earn sufficient altogether for her own maintenance. Still, if David should happen to come back with a little money to go on with, all would be well for another week or two, and some work might turn up for him.

Mrs. Fell was very lonesome without her boy, and sorely did she miss him. She was one of those mothers who think nothing of their girls in comparison with their sons; and David had always been good to her, and cheered her up when she was most downcast. She fancied he was growing like his father; and the sound of his voice or his footstep brought back the memories of happier days. David had promised to be home on Saturday, and she almost expected him on Friday night; but Friday night passed by and David was still away. During the long, sleepless hours of darkness she was thinking of him ceaselessly, little dreaming that her boy was spending his first night in gaol.

Saturday passed slowly by; and when evening came Mrs. Fell set her door ajar, and sat just within it in the dark, looking out into the lighted passage and staircase, common to all the lodgers. David would be sure to whistle as he came down the street, and her ear would catch the sound while he was still a long way off. She felt no hunger tonight, and was scarcely conscious of her pain. All her thoughts and cares were centred on her boy.

"He'd never break his promise, Bess," she said, softly; "he knows I'm hungering for a sight of him, and whatever luck he's had he's sure to come home to-night. I've wished a thousand times as I'd never let him go; but it's over now, and he shall never go again if we can only keep him from it. We'll get more washing done, you and me, won't we, Bess? And maybe David will have better luck in getting jobs to do. Oh, my lad, my lad! But he'll be here very soon now."

She checked the sobs which hindered her from hearing, and sat still for some minutes, listening with strained ears to catch his whistle amid the hubbub of sounds that noised about her. At last she sent Bess to the street-door to look up the narrow, ill-lighted street to the corner with the brilliantly illuminated spirit vaults, round which David might come any moment with the proceeds of his begging expedition. Bess had some bright visions of

In Prison and Out

her own, based upon the stories of successful beggary which the neighbours told to one another, and she was as full of impatient anticipation as her mother.

"It's almost like the time I used to watch for father, Bess, before we were wed," said Mrs. Fell, plaintively, "and I was never more on the fidgets then than I am now for Davy, poor lad! I can't keep myself still a moment, Father used to wear a plush weskit as was as soft as soft could be, and I'd dearly like Davy to have one like it. I priced one in a shop one day, but it was more than I could give when I was in full work. And, Bess, I'd like you to have a pink cotton gown, such as I was wed in; but there, it's no use to think on such things! It's God's will, and He knows best. If my lad 'ud only come in I should care for nothing."

Bess went off to the door, stepping softly past the front room, where their next neighbour, Blackett, lived, and gazed up to the stream of light shining across the road through the tavern window. She stood there for a few minutes in silence.

"He's comin', mother," cried Bess, quietly; and the poor woman's heart throbbed painfully as she leaned back against the wall almost faint from joy, whilst Bess ran eagerly up the street towards the light, which for a brief moment had irradiated the figure of her brother. But it was not David whom she met, though it was a boy of his age and size; and Bess felt near crying out aloud when she saw who it was. Still, he was an old companion and playfellow, and as nearly a friend as Blackett's son could be; for he was Roger Blackett, whose father, living in the front room on the ground-floor, close against the door through which every one went in and out, was the terror of all the inmates of the crowded house.

"Roger, have you seen our Davy anywhere?" she inquired.

"No, I haven't," he answered. "Is father in the house, Bess?"

"Ay!" she said.

"Then I'll stay outside," he went on. "He does nothing but bang me, and curse at me for an idle dog and a cowardly soft. He's drove the rest of 'em into thievin', and he'll never let me a-be till he's drove me to it. I was very near it tonight, Bess."

In Prison and Out

"Oh, don't!" she cried, "don't! I'd never do worse than beg, if I was you. I know David 'ud die afore he'd steal, and so 'ud mother. We'd all clem to death afore we'd take to thievin'".

"I'd have been drove to it long ago," said Roger, "if it hadn't been along of you and your mother, Bess. Father's always larfin' at folks like you settin' up to be honest; and he's always sayin' as I haven't got a drop of real blood in me. I'm bound to be drove to it, however long I fight shy of it. Only it 'ud vex you, Bess."

"Ah!" she answered, earnestly. "Mother 'ud never let David or me speak to you again. She's set dead agen thievin', mother is. She won't let us know any gaol–birds. You see," continued Bess, with an air of pride, "none of us has ever been in trouble—up before the justices, you know. We've never had nothink to do with the police, 'cept civility; and the police has nothink to do with us. Better starve nor steal, mother says."

But Bess had been so long in the street that Mrs. Fell's impatience had conquered her. She had crept to the street door, and was making her way painfully towards them.

"Bess, is it Davy?" she called. "Be sharp, and bring him here."

"We're coming, mother," cried Bess; "it's only Roger. You go back, and let him come into our room for a bit, for company. You come with me, Roger, and talk a bit to mother: she's frettin' after Davy so! You ask her about the parson's garden, and the place where she used to live, and anything you can think of, for a bit, till Davy comes."

The two children stole softly past the closed door of the front room, and hid themselves in the darkness of Mrs. Fell's kitchen.

"It's nobody but poor Roger," said Bess, softly. "Davy's not come yet, and Roger's afeard of his father till he gets dead drunk. Let him stay with us a bit, mother."

There had always been a dread in Mrs. Fell's mind of her children growing too intimate with Roger Blackett, whose two elder brothers were openly pursuing the successful calling of thieves, with occasional periods of absence supposed to be passed in prison; but she had been too much afraid of Blackett to forbid all intercourse with his sons. Roger was nearly fourteen, and had not been in trouble yet, so she could not very well refuse to let him enter her room.

In Prison and Out

"He's welcome," she said coldly, "as long as he keeps himself honest."

"That won't be for long," muttered Roger; "father's always a-goin' on with me to keep myself, and I've got no way o' keeping myself, save thievin'. He's getting angrier with me every day."

"But there's God 'll be angry with you if you thieve," said Mrs. Fell; "and if you make Him angry, He can do worse at you than your father. You ought to be afeard of Him."

"Where is He?" asked Roger.

"He lives in heaven, where good folks go when they die," she answered; "but He sees everything, and can do everything. Everything as happens is just what He pleases. He could make us all rich and well and happy in a moment o' time, if He chose; but it's His will we should be poor and ill and miserable, and it's all right, somehow; so we must keep still, and believe as it's all right. I know I often says, 'It's God's will,' and it seems a little better. But what I was goin' to tell you is, that God won't ever have thieves in heaven. 'There's a great pit somewhere, full of fire and brimstone, where all wicked folks go, and if you thieve you'll go there. I don't know exactly where it is, or how it is, but it's all gospel, they say. It's worse than hundreds of gaols."

The woman's low, weak, faltering voice, uttering these terrible words in the darkness, made Roger's heart shrink with a strange awe and dread. He was glad to feel Bess close beside him, and to know that she was listening as well as himself.

"God's worse than father," he said, trembling.

"No, no," continued Mrs. Fell; "I've heard folks preachin' in the streets, and some among 'em said He loves us all, somehow. I heard one of 'em saying over and over again 'God is love.' And he'd some little tickets, about as big as pawn-tickets, with those words printed plain on 'em, and he gave one to everybody as asked him. I s'pose there's some truth in it. 'God is love,' I say to myself hundreds o' times in the nights, when I lie awake for pain; and there's comfort in it. Ay, when my pains are worst, and when I'm faintin' with hunger, if I say 'God is love,' it helps me on a bit. It's all I know, and I don't know that very clear."

"Do God love everybody?" inquired Roger, anxiously.

In Prison and Out

"Yes," she answered.

"Do He love father?" he asked again.

"Yes, I s'pose so," she said in a tone of doubt.

"Then I don't believe it," went on Roger. "He didn't ought to love father; He ought to put him in that pit o' fire and brimstone, for he's a thief, and he wants to make me a thief. And if He loved any on us He'd never let us be drove to thievin' and beggin'. Folks say as Davy's gone a–beggin'. No, God loves rich folks, may be; but He don't care a rush for poor folks."

"I can't tell how it is," moaned Mrs. Fell, "only it's a comfort to me to say 'God is love,' and make believe it's true. And my Davy 'll never be a thief, Roger—never! If folks do say he's gone a–beggin', they can't say worse of him. Ah, I wish he'd only come!"

But though she and Bess sat up till long after midnight, and until every inmate of the overcrowded tenement had returned to their miserable dens, and there was not a sound to drown the echo of any footstep coming down the street, there was still no sign of David's coming. Bess fell asleep at last on the floor at her mother's feet; but she kept awake, shivering with cold and pain, and heart–sick with vague terrors as to what should keep the boy away.

As day after day passed on, bringing no tidings of David, the mother's anguish of soul grew almost intolerable. It seemed to overmaster her bodily pain, and render her nearly insensible to it. Every morning she wandered about, asking news of her boy from everybody who had ever known him, until her strength was worn out, and then she would stand for hours, leaning against the wall at the street corner, looking along the road, and straining her eyes to catch some glimpse of him amid the ever–changing stream of people passing by. She could no longer bring herself to stand at her washing–tub, cheating the parish by earning a few extra pence for herself by the toil of her hands. Little by little all that was left of her few possessions found their way to the familiar pawn–shop, till her room was as bare of furniture as it was possible to be, and yet be a human dwelling–place.

There was one treasure she had never parted with, however pressing and bitter her necessities had been through her long years of widowhood. It was the one possession which had been the pride of her heart. This was her wedding-ring, of good solid gold, bought for her, and placed upon her hand by the husband she had lost ten years ago. She had been too careful of it to wear it while at work; but every evening and every Sunday her children had been used to see the golden glitter of it on her finger, and to regard it with a sort of reverential delight. It was the visible sign to them of their dead father, and of the good times their mother could tell them of, but which they had not known themselves. They had gone to bed many a night supperless, that they might keep the mother's ring from the pawn-shop, and run no risk of losing it.

But things had come to such a pass during David's absence, that the ring must go. It was still little worn, not much thinner than when David Fell, the carpenter, had wedded his young wife with it. Next to any grief or calamity befalling her children, this was the sharpest trial Mrs. Fell could undergo. Bess helped her to crawl to the pawnbroker's shop—for she would not trust it even to Bess—and she laid it down on the counter with a pang nearly heart-breaking. The pawnbroker fastened a number to it, gave her a ticket, and pushed a few shillings towards her.

"Take care of it!" she cried with vehement urgency in her tone—" take care of it. I shall redeem it; God in heaven knows I shall redeem it some day. It's God's will!" she sobbed, her dim, eager eyes following it as the pawnbroker opened a drawer, and dropped it carelessly among a heap of pledges similar to it.

Chapter 4. OLD EUCLID'S HOARD

As Mrs. Fell, leaning heavily on the arm of Bess, crept homeward after her sorrowful visit to the pawnbroker, they saw an old man, one of their neighbours, making his way with a shambling and limping tread along the uneven pavement before them. The lamps were lit down the narrow and dirty street, and the light fell on the dingy figure of the old man as he passed under them, with his stooping shoulders and his long ragged locks of grey hair falling below his battered and broken hat, round which still clung a little band of black material that had become nearly brown with rain and sunshine. He was a small man, and seemed to have withered and shrunk into a more meagre thinness than when his clothes had been bought, now many years ago. The face under the battered hat was of a

In Prison and Out

yellow brownness and much wrinkled, with shaggy eyebrows hanging over his eyes. There was a gleam in these dim and sunken eyes, as if it was possible for him to smile, but the possibility seldom became a fact. He looked half asleep as he shuffled along, and in a low husky voice he was dreamily crying cresses, but not at all as though he expected any one of his neighbours to spend a penny on his perishable stock.

"There's poor old Euclid!" said Mrs. Fell in a tone of pity, as if she was looking at one whose circumstances were as bad, if not worse, than her–own.

The old man's Christian name was Euclid, his surname Jones, but in the multitude of Joneses the latter had long been lost, and was almost forgotten. He was the son of a village schoolmaster in some quiet spot in Wales, who had called his only child Euclid, with a vague and distant hope of seeing him some day a distinguished mathematical scholar. But the schoolmaster and his wife had both died before little Euclid had fairly mastered the alphabet, and from that time he had lived among the neighbours, now with one and now with another, passing from cottage to cottage, until he was old enough to scare crows and tend pigs. Little learning did Euclid get at these early employments. In course of time he drifted up to London, where he worked on the roads till he was disabled by an accident. He had married a wife who bore him eight children, born and bred under every chance against health and life, and dying, all but one, just as they grew old enough to do something for themselves, after they had tested their father's love and endurance to the utmost. His wife was dead also. He had buried them all in their own coffins, unassisted by the parish, a remembrance which stirred up his downcast heart with a feeling of honest pride whenever it crossed his brain.

Life had brought to Euclid an enigma to solve, stiffer and more intricate than the most abstruse mathematical problem—how to keep himself and his off the parish during life, and how to get buried when all was over without the same dreaded and degrading aid. The problem was but partially solved yet; there still remained his youngest child and himself to die, and be buried.

Euclid turned in at the same door as that to which Mrs. Fell was painfully creeping. He lived in the one attic of the house, having the advantage over Mrs. Fell in more light and fresher air, and in the quietness of a storey to himself. But he possessed few other advantages. His household goods were as poor as hers had been before all that was worth pawning had gone to the pawn–shop. The fireplace consisted of three bars of iron let into

In Prison and Out

the chimney, with a brick on each side for a bob, on one of which stood a brown earthenware tea-pot simmering at the spout, as if the tea had been boiling for some time. There was a bed on the floor close by the handful of fire, and Euclid's first glance fell upon it; but it was empty, for a sickly looking girl of eighteen was sitting on a broken chair before the fire, cowering over it with outstretched hands. She had wrapped herself in an old shawl, and was holding it tightly about her, as though she felt the chill of the November evening; but she smiled brightly when the old man's wrinkled face and dim eyes met her gaze, as he stood in the doorway an instant, looking anxiously and sadly at her.

"Come in, daddy, and shut the door," she said cheerfully. "I'm not bad to-day; but you're late—later than ever. It's gone six, and I thought you would never, never come."

"Folks did not care to buy creases this cold day," he answered, his husky voice striving to soften itself into tenderness; "but Victoria, my dear, you've not waited tea for me?"

"I should think I have," she said, rising from the only chair, and compelling him with all her little strength to sit down on it, while she took an old box for her seat. "I couldn't relish the best o' tea alone at this time o' night and you in the streets, daddy. So we'll have it at once, for it's been made oh! hours ago—at least it's near an hour by the clock. That clock's real company to me, father," she added, looking proudly at a little loud-ticking clock against the wall, which seemed the best and busiest thing in the bare room.

"I ain't got no 'erring for you, Victoria," he said regretfully, "nor nothing else for a relish—nothing save a few creases, and they'd be too cold for your stomach, my dear. If you feel set on anything, I'll take a penny or two from our little store, you know. It's all quite safe, isn't it, my dear?"

"Yes, yes," she answered, a shadow flitting across her face for a moment; "you needn't never be afeard of that not being safe. But I'm not set on anything, daddy."

"How much is it now, Victoria?" he inquired, his eyes glistening a little as he listened eagerly to her reply.

"It's two pound sixteen shilling and ninepence three farthings," she answered, without hesitation.

In Prison and Out

"I take good care of it."

"I think we shall do it, Victoria," he said, with an air of satisfaction; "and after that, my dear, there will be nobody but me, and I'm not afeard but I'll save enough for that. No, no; I shouldn't like any on us to die like a scamp, on the parish, and be buried in a parish coffin."

Victoria had been reaching down the two cracked cups and the loaf of bread from a corner cupboard, and now she stood for a moment looking wistfully into the fire, her pale thin face flushed a little into almost delicate beauty. Under the pillow on which she rested her head every night, and on which it–lay many a long hour of the wearful day, there was always hidden a precious little store of money, slowly accumulating by a few pence at a time—the fund that was to pay for her own coffin and the other costs of her poor funeral. She had made a shroud of coarse calico for herself, and kept it carefully ready against the time it would be needed. There was no question in her mind or her father's that this fund would be needed, probably before the next summer came. Her doctor, who was a druggist living in the next street, assured her that good living, and better clothing, and warmer lodging were all she needed; but he–might as well have ordered her to the south of France for the winter. It was Euclid's chief anxiety now that the sum should grow as fast as possible, lest an unusually severe winter might hasten on the necessity for it. And to Victoria it was a matter of as much interest and care as to him, so often did she reckon up the cost of a coffin and a grave, and count over the money provided to procure them for her. She thought of it again as she stood looking into the fire, and saw as vividly and fleetly as a flash of lightning her own funeral passing down the narrow, common staircase, with the children trooping after it, but only her old and weeping father following as mourner. She stooped down and kissed him, as if to comfort him beforehand for the grief that was to come.

"Is anythink ailin' you, Victoria?" he inquired in as gentle a tone as he could lower his voice to.

"Nothin' fresh, daddy," she answered; "only you'll be lonesome when I'm gone."

"Ay, ay," said Euclid. "It'll be a dark shop wi'out you, my dear."

In Prison and Out

He said no more, but sat slowly rubbing his hands up and down his legs before the fire, while his memory travelled back over the twenty-five years that had passed since he was a strong man, able and willing to work hard and to live hard for the sake of his wife and children. Victoria saw him counting his children on his fingers, as he huskily muttered their names. He seemed to see them all, his boys and girls, who were gone out of this troublesome world down into the dark secret of the grave; they were all living in his memory. And his wife, too, who had trodden the same strange yet familiar road eighteen years ago. He had buried them all, and had never once taken a penny from the parish. His withered face lit up as the thought crossed his mind.

"Victoria," he said, as if this recollection had reminded him of Mrs. Fell, "there's a mort o' trouble downstairs in the ground-floor back. There's Mrs. Fell as bad off or worse than us, though she do take parish pay. There's no luck in parish money, I know; but she was dead beat, I s'pose. I saw her comin' back from the pawnshop, and she looked like death. There's her boy David away, and nobody knows where he's gone to, and she's almost heartbroke. I took the liberty o' noticin' and there's not a scrap o' fire in their room. So, Victoria, my dear, if you didn't mind it, we might ask her up here a bit when we've done our tea. There's not enough for all, or we'd ask her to come up for her tea. But she's got no fire, and we have, and four of us will be warmer than two, if you didn't mind it."

"Mind it, daddy?" repeated Victoria. "I'd be right glad, if she'll come."

Many a time had Victoria glanced longingly into Mrs. Fell's room, as she passed the door, and wished she would call out and invite her in. But Mrs. Fell had felt herself in a superior position to Euclid—a laundress being surely of a higher social standing than a water-cress seller, to say nothing of living on the ground-floor instead of the attic—and she had taken but little notice of Euclid's girl amid the constantly changing lodgers who inhabited the house. Bess was better known to Victoria; and David had many a time shown himself friendly, and run errands for her when she was too poorly to go out herself. To-night she could not swallow a morsel after her father's suggestion. As soon as tea was over and the cups and tea-pot put away, with every token of their poor meal, Euclid went downstairs to carry his invitation in person, whilst Victoria arranged an empty box or two to serve as seats about the fire, upon which she put another tiny shovelful of coals. Her colour came and went fitfully, as she heard Mrs. Fell's slow footstep mounting the steps leading to their attic, followed by her father and Bess, and she received them shyly, but gladly, at the door.

In Prison and Out

"It's very kind on you and Mr. Euclid, I'm sure," panted Mrs. Fell, with the ghost of a smile on her face, "and I take it neighbourly, and if there's anything as me and Bess can do—"

"Please come and sit down in the chair," said Victoria, interrupting her easily, for she was still struggling for breath. She was soon seated in the chair, which was placed in front of the fire, whilst Euclid sat on one side on an old box, with Bess and Victoria opposite on another. The flickering flame of the small fire shone upon their faces, and was the only light by which they saw each other. But in a few minutes they felt almost like old friends.

"She's the last I've got," said old Euclid to Mrs. Fell, nodding at Victoria, who was talking to Bess "her mother died on her, when she were born eighteen years ago. She were too weak to get the better on it, and she had to go. I'd five little children when she died. Victoria's got her complaint," he went on, in a lower tone, "and she's the last out o' eight on them. Boys and gals, they're all gone afore me."

"It's His will as knows best, Mr. Euclid," said Mrs. Fell, with a heavy sigh.

"I s'pose it is," replied Euclid. "I hope He knows, for I'm sure I don't. I've had no time for thinkin' of nothink but how to keep off the parish. Not as I'd say a word agen a woman takin' parish pay; a poor weakly woman like you. But it 'ud be a sore disgrace for a man to come on the parish, even for his buryin'".

Mrs. Fell sighed again, and sat looking into the red embers of the fire sadly, as if she was seeing again the bright days of her married life.

"I never lost nobody save my poor David, my husband, I mean," she said, "and by good luck he were in a buryin' club, and they gave him a very good funeral; a hearse, and a mournin' coach for me and the two children, and plumes! But there'll be nobody save the parish to bury me; for Bess is only a child, and David's gone."

"Where's he gone to?" asked Victoria.

"He went out on a little journey nigh upon a month ago," she answered, "and we've never heard a word of him since he said 'Good–bye, mother.' He's never come back again. Somethink's happened to him I know; for he's always that good to me and Bess, you

In Prison and Out

couldn't think! I'm frettin' after him all the while more than I can tell; it's wastin' me away. But it's God's will, as good folks say; and there's none on us as can fight agen Him."

"And Bess says you've been forced to part wi' your weddin'–ring," Victoria replied, with a shy look of sympathy.

The tears welled up into Mrs. Fell's eyes, and Bess bowed her head in shame. For the first evening in her life when she had no work to do, the poor woman felt that her finger had lost its precious sign of her married life. She might almost as well have been an unmarried woman; one of those wretched creatures on whom she had always looked down with honest pride, and a little hardness. She laid her right hand over her undecorated finger, and looked back into Victoria's sympathising face with an expression of bitter grief.

"I'll work till I drop to get it back," cried Bess, with energy.

"I wish my missis were alive now," said Euclid. "I'm always a wishin' it; but she were a good woman, and she knew summat more about God than most folks; and about Him as died for us. I never was a scholar, but she could read, ay, splendid! and she knew a mort o' things. She taught me a lot, and I remembered them long enough to teach Victoria some of 'em. Victoria, my dear, there's them verses as was your mother's favourites; them as I taught you when you was little. I've forgot 'em myself, Mrs. Fell; but she's got them all right and straight in her head, and she says them back to me now my memory's gone. Sometimes I think it's her mother a sayin' of 'em.

'The Lord,' you know, my dear."

Victoria's face flushed again, and her voice trembled a little as she began to speak, whilst Bess fastened her dark eyes eagerly upon her; and Euclid and Mrs. Fell, with their careworn and withered faces turned straight to the fire, nodded their heads at the close of each verse as if uttering a silent Amen.

"The Lord is my Shepherd; I shall not want.
"He maketh me to lie down in green pastures:
He leadeth me beside the still waters.

"He restoreth my soul: He leadeth me in the paths of righteousness for His name's sake.

"Yea, though I walk through the valley of the shadow of death, I will fear no evil: for Thou art with me; Thy rod and Thy staff they comfort me.

"Thou preparest a table before me in the presence of mine enemies: Thou anointest my head with oil; my cup runneth over.

"Surely goodness and mercy shall follow me all the days of my life: and I will dwell in the house of the Lord for ever."

Chapter 5. LESSONS IN PRISON

It was quite dark at night when the prison van containing David and other convicted offenders reached the gaol to which they were committed. As yet he was still feeling bewildered and confused, and the sound of heavy doors clanging after him as he passed along them, and the long narrow passages through which he was led, only served to heighten his perplexity. He had hardly ever been within walls, except those of the poor house which had been his home as long as he could remember; and the prison appeared immeasurably large, as he dragged his weary footsteps along the stone flagging of the corridors. The spotless cleanliness of both floor and walls seemed also to remove him altogether out of the world with which he was acquainted. The dirt and squalor of the old gaols would have been more homelike to him. By the time his hair had been cropped close to his head, and the prison garb put upon him in the place of his own familiar clothes, stained and tattered with long wear of them, he began to doubt his own identity. Was he really David Fell? Could he be the boy who had hitherto led the freest life possible, roaming about the busy streets, with no person to forbid or to question him? David Fell could not be he who was now locked up, quite alone, in a little cell, dimly lighted by a gas–jet, which itself was locked up in a cage lest he should touch it. Not a sound came to his ears, let him listen as sharply as he could. Where was the old roll and roar of the streets, and the cries of children, and the shrill voices of women, and the din, and tumult, and stir, and life to which he was accustomed? No dream as dreadful as this silence and solitude had ever visited him.

For a long while he could not go to sleep, though his previous night in the police station had been one of wakefulness. His hammock was comfortable, more comfortable than any bed he had ever slept on; and his prison rug was warm. But the very comfort and warmth brought his mother to his mind, his mother and little Bess. What were they doing now?

In Prison and Out

Were they shivering on their chard mattress, under their threadbare counterpane, which was all that was left to them to keep out the night's chill? Perhaps they were looking out for him. What day was it? Was it not Saturday to-day? And he had promised to be home on Saturday!

Oh! how different it would all have been if he had only escaped being caught! He would have been at home by this time; and now they could have had a bit of fire in the grate, and something to make a feast of as they sat round it, whilst he told the story of his wanderings, and tried to describe all the rich, good folks who had been kind to him. Or if the magistrate had taken away all the money, and let him go home on his promise never to go begging again, even that would have been nothing to this trouble. He fancied he could see his mother's face, pale yet smiling, as she listened to his danger and his escape from it, and Bess sitting on the floor, with shining eyes and clasped hands, hearkening eagerly to every word. Why had they sent him to gaol? At last he sobbed himself to sleep; but all through the night might be heard, if there had been an ear to hear, the heavy deep-drawn sob of the boy's overwhelmed heart.

He was awakened early in the morning, and briefly told what he must do before quitting his cell. Then he ate his breakfast alone in the dreary solitude of the prison walls, and the food almost choked him. It seemed to the boy, used to the wild, utter freedom of the streets, as if his very limbs were fettered, and that he could not move either hand or foot freely. His body did not seem to belong to himself any longer. He was neither hungry nor cold, as he might have been at home, but his head ached and his heart was sore with thoughts of his mother; he was unutterably sick and sad. Cold and hunger were almost like familiar friends to him; but he did not know this faintness and heaviness, this numbness which kept him chained to the prison seat, and made it appear an impossibility that a day or two ago he was rambling about as long as he pleased, and where he pleased, in the wide, free world outside the prison walls. Were there any boys like him still running, and leaping, and shouting out yonder in the autumn sunshine?

It was Sunday morning, and he was left longer than usual to himself. He was taken to the chapel, and sat in his place during the reading of the prayers and the sermon which followed; but not a word penetrated to his bewildered brain. It was much the same on the week-day when he went to school. He knew a little both of reading and writing; but he could not control his attention to make use of what he knew. He said the alphabet stupidly, and wrote his first copy of straight lines badly. He could not bring himself to

In Prison and Out

think of these things. His mind was wandering sadly round the central thought that he was in gaol, and what would become of his mother and little Bess without him.

David was naturally a bright boy, active in mind and body, but he was crushed by the sudden and extreme penalty that had befallen him. He had all along known that the police were "down" upon begging, but it had not entered his mind that he could ever actually get into gaol except for thieving. Among the street lads of his acquaintance many a one had been in for some short term for picking pockets or stealing from the street stalls; but few of these had ever been sentenced to three months' imprisonment. And he had always kept his hands from picking and stealing—the only item of his duty to man which his mother had impressed upon him. He would not have begged if he could have worked; but no man of the hundreds and thousands about him had offered him work, or seen that he was taught to work. Yet here he was for three months in gaol, a lad who had never known any will to guide him but his own untrained and vagrant nature, and his mother's kindly but weak indulgence.

The first glimmer of hope came to him when he was set to learn shoemaking. This was a trade by which he could earn a living—not the trade he would have chosen; his ambition was to be a carpenter like his unknown father—but still honest real work. He received his first lesson in a handicraft with ardour, and sat with an old boot on his knee, picking it to pieces with unwearying industry. If he could only learn as much as to mend his mother's shoes before his term was out! The tears started to his dull, bloodshot eyes, and his lips quivered at the thought of it. He would do his best at any rate to learn this lesson.

The gaol was a large one, and the number of prisoners great. David had been asked if he was a Roman Catholic—a question he did not understand, and could not answer. He was, therefore, classed with the Protestants, and put under the care of the gaol chaplain, who saw him among the other prisoners, and taught him his duty towards God in a class, but who could not find time to give him any individual attention. The chaplain told him, among the rest, that he had broken the laws of his country and of God, and that his punishment was the just reward of his sin. David's ideas of right and wrong were exceedingly limited, and his conscience very uninformed; but he could not believe he had done wrong; and he did not. His mother was starving and he had begged for help. If the laws of his country and of God forbade him to do this, they were in the wrong.

In Prison and Out

He could not have put his thoughts into words, but they were none the less in his heart—dim, bewildering, and oppressive; and he pondered over them night and day. Very few persons spoke to him, and he was never ready to speak in reply. Those who taught him thought him a blockhead, or fancied that he was at least shamming incapacity and vacancy of mind. As a matter of fact his mind was always absent, except at his cobbling lesson, for he was incessantly brooding over the recollection of his free life, and of the poor desolate home he had been so suddenly torn from.

David had no idea of writing to his mother, or hearing from her. No such thing as a letter reaching them, or being written in their home, had ever occurred within his memory. The policeman was a much more frequent visitor than the postman in their street. Yet he longed for her to know where he was. Day after day he wondered what had happened to her and Bess, and knew they were wondering and fretting about him. The only comfort he had, the only miserable spark of hope, was in thinking he should know how to mend their shoes when he went home.

It was, therefore, with a sudden burst as of sunshine that he learned one day that prisoners might write to their friends once in three months. The schoolmaster gave him the writing materials, and he took unwearied pains over a letter to his mother. The sheet of note-paper contained the address of the gaol, and under it David wrote, in his crooked, ill-formed characters, as follows:-

"Dear Mother,—I was took up for begging, and sent to jal, and I'm lernin' to mend shoes. Don't yu fret about me. I luv yu and Bess. They'll let me out in 3 months, and I'll mend yure shoos. I've kep my hands from pickin' and steelin' as muther ses. God bless you. From david fell yure luvin' son."

He slept that night more soundly than he had ever done before within the prison walls, and dreamed pleasant dreams of working for his mother, and buying her and little Bess all they needed with the money he had earned.

Chapter 6. NOT GOD'S WILL?

When Mrs. Fell and Bess bade Euclid and Victoria good-night, and went downstairs to their own room, they felt cheered and comforted by the neighbourliness they had

In Prison and Out

received. Bess was ready to declare Victoria the prettiest and cleverest girl in the world. As they opened the door they saw a letter lying just within it, which had been slipped through the nick below it, and which was scarcely visible in the darkness. Such an extraordinary event, one which had never befallen them before, filled them with so much astonishment that it was with trembling hands Bess stooped to pick it up. It was a real letter, with a stamp and postmark upon it, though they could hardly believe their own eyes. There was no light in their own room, not even a dim farthing candle to burn, and there was no resource but to carry the strange letter to the gaslight on the stairs, and read it there as quickly and quietly as possible, with the very probable chance of some of their neighbours coming by and watching them inquisitively.

It must be news of David; there was no one else in the world to write to them. Bess could not read writing, and it was no easy task to Mrs. Fell. But as soon as she unfolded the sheet of paper, which was headed by the name of the gaol where he was imprisoned printed plainly upon it, and which she read half aloud before the meaning reached her brain, she uttered a piercing shriek of anguish, which rang through the whole house, and brought every inmate of it running into the passages and upon the staircases. Mrs. Fell was lying in a deep swoon upon the floor, and Bess was kneeling beside her, calling to her and trying to raise her up. Blackett was the first to reach her, and the half-drunken man gave her a rough push with his foot, uttering a brutal oath.

"You leave her alone!" cried old Euclid, hurrying downstairs, and confronting Blackett with a courage that astonished himself, when he came to think of it; "you leave Mrs. Fell be! She's been spendin' the evenin' with me and my daughter, and I'll take care on her. You ain't no man if you'd kick a poor sickly woman like her. You're a coward if you touch her again, and I say so. Ain't he?" he shouted in his hoarse voice, as he turned with a quivering face and excited gestures to the cluster of neighbours gathered about them.

"Ay, he is!" cried the crowd with so unanimous a voice that even Blackett was cowed by it, and, contenting himself with muttering some bad language, retreated to his own place. Two or three of the neighbours helped Euclid to carry the poor woman into her room. Even to them, used to destitution as they were, it seemed bare of everything. There was no seat left, unless a few bricks, picked up in the street, could be called seats; and they had to lay her down upon the bare sacking of the bedsteads, from which the bed and clothing had all disappeared. Euclid gazed round him with a strange pity stirring at his heart, mingled with a sense of superior comfort in his own circumstances. He felt almost

In Prison and Out

like a rich man.

"This is bad, worse than any on us," he said; "and she might ha' been my widow, if I'd died first, instead of my wife. She might ha' been the widow of any one on you. I vote as we make a little collection for her in th' house, and I'll begin with a shillin', and that's more than I've earned to-day. Some on you can do it easier than me."

"She gets four shillings and eightpence, parish pay, every Tuesday," objected one of the women who stood by.

"And pays arf-a-crown a week rent," replied Euclid; "it's short-commons after that."

" She's always a-hungered," sobbed Bess; "nothin' can satisfy mother."

"She ought to go into the house, where she'd have medicine and everythink," said another voice; "the orficer says so."

"Who says she ought to go into the house?" asked Euclid, lifting up his head and looking round him with eyes almost bright with indignation. "She as is a decent, hard-workin' woman, and a honest man's widow! She's not the sort as goes into the house. We know who goes there—bad women as no decent man 'ud look at, and drunken women, and swearin', cursin' women. There couldn't be worse folks in hell, and I'd as lief say she ought to go to hell; the company 'ud be as good. Don't nobody speak o' goin' to the house while I'm by."

Old Euclid had always been regarded by his neighbours as a quiet, timid old man, who hadn't a word to cast at a dog. There was something so unusual both in his vehement words and his excited gestures that, one by one, they slunk out of the miserable room in silence, leaving him and Bess to the task of bringing back the fainting woman to consciousness. She was still clutching the letter convulsively in her fingers, but as Bess opened them to chafe the palms of her cold hands, it fluttered down upon the floor. Euclid picked it up, and carried it to the light of the candle which somebody had brought in and left upon the chimney-piece.

"Who's it from?" asked Bess, anxiously. "Is it from Davy?"

In Prison and Out

"Ah! 'David Fell, your lovin' son,'" he read; "but it comes from gaol! He's in gaol!"

Euclid's grey old head dropped, and his voice sank into a hoarse murmur. It was no longer a wonder to him that Mrs. Fell had fallen into a death-like swoon. The workhouse was terrible; but the gaol was a lower depth still. He stood silent for a few minutes thinking. David had always been a sort of favourite with him; he liked his bright boyish face, and his merry whistle as he stepped briskly about. And the lad had often carried his basket for him, and shouted "Cresses" with his clear young voice, when his own throat was dry and husky with crying them all day about the streets. But now David Fell was a gaol-bird!

Presently there came to his ear the feeble murmur of his name from David's mother, and he hastened to her side, looking down on her ashy face with a strange gentleness in his sunken eyes.

"Please read it up loud," she said, in a laborious whisper, as if she had scarcely strength to form the words with her trembling lips. Euclid read the few lines in a measured voice, giving every word its fullest length; and then he folded it up again, and laid it down near the mother's hand.

"It's only for beggin'!" he cried, "three months for beggin' for his mother! God help us all! There's something wrong somewhere! Them justices must have hearts like mine, I s'pose, yet they sent Davy to gaol for three months for beggin' for his mother. If they'd only take the time for to see what they'd done! But there, they don't take the time; or they'd never punish a lad like David, the son of a decent, hard-workin' woman, as was left a widow with two children to keep. God help us all!"

"It's only for beggin'!" murmured Mrs. Fell, with tears streaming down her cheeks, "only for beggin'!"

"Don't you take on too much," urged Euclid, "he'll come home all right, and I'll look after the lad for you."

But it was hard for Mrs. Fell to comfort herself about David. It was no uncommon event for boys in their street to get into gaol; but it was almost always for stealing, and she knew no one would believe that David had been sent there for begging only. How

In Prison and Out

Blackett would glory and triumph in it! His elder sons were known to be thieves, and he was constantly pushing and urging Roger towards the same course, in the hope of getting him off his hands. Yet it had never once crossed her mind that her own boy Davy could ever be in prison. His father had been an honest, industrious artisan, priding himself on never touching his neighbour's goods by so much as a finger; and she had not thought of David failing, under any stress of temptation, to follow in his steps. David was no thief; but still he was in gaol! She kept murmuring to herself, "It's only for beggin'!" But was the bitterness lessened to her that her only son had met with such a penalty for so slight a fault? He would come out into the world branded as if he had been a thief, with the shame of a gaol clinging to him through the rest of his life. And she herself had always held up her head among the neighbours. How could she bear to be pointed at as the mother of a gaol-bird? The pain was more than she could bear.

Euclid and Victoria were very good to her in her fresh trouble, and helped her as far as their means allowed; the little store of money for Victoria's burial suffering thereby. Many of the neighbours, too, thought of her, and brought her from time to time a morsel of their own not over-abundant food. Even Blackett offered her help, which she turned away from with a sick heart. She was not quite so starved and friendless as she had been before her desperate circumstances were discovered, but she felt more heartbroken, and there was none to comfort her. Victoria repeated her hymns and verses to her, but they seemed words without meaning in her great sorrow. She had set before her one aim, to see her children start in life, honest and blameless, as their father had been before them. Night and day she had toiled and denied herself to this end. She had given herself no rest, but had struggled on through grievous pain and in great darkness of spirit; and she had failed. The hard battle had been fought, and she was conquered.

"Davy 'ud have made a good man," she moaned to herself, through the long, sleepless nights, as she thought of him in gaol; "he'd have growed up like his father, if I could ha' kep' up another two-three years. It's come too soon on me. But now he's got a sully and a stain on him as 'll never wash off, live as long as live he may. He's been in gaol, folks 'll say. And whatever 'ill become o' Bess if Davy goes wrong? He'd have kep' her up, if he'd been a good man. Oh, Lord! he'd have made a good man, only for this! And now he's in gaol!"

Bess was all that was left to her, and she could scarcely bear to let her go out of her sight. Blackett, who swore and raged at every one else, was beginning to speak kindly to Bess, and this filled the heart of the poor dying mother with unutterable terror. She had often been proud of her child's dark eyes and pretty hair, and thought of her own face when David Fell was courting her.

Oh! if Davy was but at home again, always with Bess, unconsciously shielding her from untold dangers! Suppose even that she died before Davy's time was up! If she should never, never see her boy's face again! And to leave Bess alone, quite alone!

It would have been a hard and bitter sorrow to leave her children, if she had had a good hope of their doing well; but oh! how infinitely harder and more bitter it was to die while David was in gaol, and when Blackett was speaking kindly to little Bess!

Once she tried to say, "It's God's will, and He knows best," but something seemed to stop her. She could not utter the words, even to her own heart.

Chapter 7. BESS BEGINS BUSINESS

Bess had not forgotten that the redemption of her mother's wedding–ring rested upon her, and that she had pledged herself to get it out of pawn. She tried in various ways to get some work to do, but she had neither strength nor skill to make her work valuable. At last she took council with Victoria, who proposed to her to go out selling water–cresses like her father; and he offered to take her with him to the market where he bought his daily supply, and start her on a beat of her own, apart from his, as he could not afford to divide his customers and his profits. A few pence, a few halfpence even, would set her up in this line of business; and with luck she might earn sufficient to keep herself and redeem the ring. But it must be done in secret lest the relieving officer should hear of it, and her mother's allowance from the parish be reduced or perhaps taken off altogether.

It may be pleasant to rise at four o'clock in June, and quitting the thick and nauseous atmosphere of the overcrowded and unventilated dwelling–place, to escape into the sweet dewy freshness of the early morning, which, even in the streets, is scented with the breath of country hay–carts and blossoming gardens; but four o'clock on a winter's morning, when Bess hurriedly dressed herself, without a light, in the thin and tattered clothes which were all she had, and thrust her naked feet into her mother's old boots; and, kissing her mother, who must lie still and lonely till she came back, stepped out into the half slush, half frost of the pavement, and the biting air—this was a sharp test of her endurance. But Euclid was waiting for her with his basket, and she trudged along at his side through the slush and the frost, carrying an old battered tea-tray a neighbour, who could be trusted with the secret, had lent her the night before. It was nearly three miles to the market. Early as the hour was, and dark as midnight still, life had begun again at the East End; and many a shivering fellow-being, shuffling along the slippery pavement, and maintaining a sombre silence, passed them like ghosts. Bess had never been out at this hour before, and she kept close to Euclid's side.

The old man was silent; for he felt put out by the presence of a companion. For twenty-five years, ever since he had recovered partially from the accident that disabled him as a labourer, he had taken this walk alone, through summer and winter; and it was bewildering to him to hear the light footsteps of Bess pattering beside him. He had so long lived altogether without intercourse with his neighbours, that he was surprised, and not altogether pleased, to find himself taking an interest in Mrs. Fell, and David, and Bess. Might not such an interest come between him and the sole aim of his life? For if he yielded too much to the stirrings of compassion and pity in his heart, some danger might arise to his slowly accumulated hoard, now lying safely under Victoria's head.

Yet Euclid felt that he could not stand by and see his neighbour die of starvation under his very eyes. No, no; that could never be. He glanced at Bess, as they passed beneath a lamp, and caught a half-smile of trustfulness in him shining in her eyes, like the look of his little children, dead long ago, who had been used to run to meet him when they heard his foot on the stairs. They were all gone to heaven now, where his wife was. He had no idea of heaven, beyond a vague fancy dwelling in his brain that there would be somewhere, out of the world or in the world he did not know, a little cottage on a hillside, such as the early home he dimly remembered, where they would all live together again, and where there would be no winter, and no more hunger or sorrow; no parish pay, and no workhouse. His lost wife would be young again, and all his children little ones; and there would be a garden for him to work in, lying round the cottage. That was Euclid's heaven.

He was still dreaming of it when they reached the market, and joined a crowd of old folks and young children waiting for the gates to be opened. It was not yet five o'clock, and the yellow glare of a few gas lamps shed a dim light upon the scene. The crowd was very quiet and subdued. All who were there were feeble folk, and did not care to waste their

In Prison and Out

strength in noise and pushing. As each old person or little child came, they took their place as near to the gate as they could get, and most of them sank into silent waiting. The poorest of the decent poor were there; those who were willing to struggle to the bitter end to earn an honest living, and keep out of the workhouse. Euclid did as the rest, and with Bess beside him, stood in patient muteness till he could make his purchases for the day.

As soon as the gates were opened there was a quiet crush through them. Euclid took more care in buying a stock of cresses for Bess than for himself; though he was fastidious in his choice, passing from hamper to hamper, and peering closely at the green leaves to detect any specks upon them. As soon as his purchases were made, he hurried Bess away to the steps of a church close by, where he showed her how to make up her bunches, and slung the old tray round her neck by a bit of cord he drew out of his pocket.

"Now, we must be as sharp as needles and pins," he said. "I've heard somewhere of a early bird as picked up a early worm. Folks 'ill be gettin' their breakfasses soon, and we must be in time to catch 'em at it. Don't you waste your time along the bettermost streets, Bess, but stick to the courts, and the mewses, and the streets where workin' men live. Rich folks ain't thinkin' o' gettin' out o' bed yet; and they don't eat creases for breakfast, but ham and eggs, and hot things. Mewses are good places in general. Walk pretty slow, two mile an hour; and keep your eye on the doors and windows for fear somebody's beckonin' at you. There now! I'll stand at the end o' this here street, and hearken how you can cry 'Creases! Fresh water–creases!' till you're out o' my sight."

Euclid stood watching Bess, with her trayful of cresses, as she paced slowly along the street, her clear, pleasant voice singing, rather than crying, the familiar words. Then he turned away with a heavy sigh. His own voice sounded husky and hollow in his ears as he shambled along his customary beat, drawling mournfully, "Cre–she! cre–she!" He felt an older man than usual; as though some additional burden of years had suddenly fallen upon his bent shoulders and bowed–down head. Yet he was only in his sixtieth year, and there was much work and much power of endurance left in him still. He had never quite starved as much as he could; and his old clothing had never been as utterly tattered as they might be. But he saw depths of poverty below even him; and for once–his heart felt heavy enough to sink him and Victoria into those lowest deeps.

"The parish!" he muttered to himself, half aloud, as he rested his dry throat for a minute or two, "the parish! And be parted from her! Not bury Victoria in her own coffin, like the rest of 'em! The parish! God help these old legs o' mine!

As if some new strength had been breathed into him, Euclid started on again, crying his street cry with more energy than before; the thought of the parish having run like a stimulant through his whole frame. He had more luck than usual, and sold so many bunches of cresses that he felt justified in buying one of the best of Yarmouth bloaters, which he chose with close cautiousness, as if he was difficult to please, at a shop he passed on his way home. It was for a relish for Victoria's tea, more than for himself. He had made as much as two shillings by his day's toil and his ten miles' tramp through the slushy streets; and after he had taken enough for the day's food and rent, there was as much as ninepence to put by.

"Let us look over our little store," he said, when their leisurely tea was ended.

He was counting up the silver and copper coins on the empty soap-box, turned on end, which served as a table when it was not wanted as a seat, when a low knock was heard at the door. There was neither lock nor latch upon it, the sole fastening being a stick passed through a staple and hold-fast within. But there was no other room in the roof, and the steep ladder-like staircase was seldom trodden by any one but themselves. Euclid made haste to gather the money into the handkerchief that usually held it, before Victoria opened the door. But Bess, who was the untimely visitor, had already seen the heap of coins through a chink in the old door, and heard their jingle as Euclid swept them out of sight. She stood thunderstruck on the door-sill, gazing in with large wide-open eyes.

"What is it, Bess?" asked Victoria.

"Oh! mother's sent me up to say as I've had good luck," she stammered, "and it's thanks to you, Mr. Euclid; and oh! please may I go again tomorrow morning?"

Ay, child," answered Euclid shortly.

Bess went downstairs with a far slower step than she had gone up. Never in her life had she seen so much money at one time, as when she had put her eye to the chink in the door, and peeped in on her friends. It seemed to her as if the whole end of the soap-box had been covered with it. Mr. Euclid, in spite of his old clothing and his poor attic, was then a rich man! If such riches could be made by selling water-cresses, then she too was on the high road to be rich. Already, to-day, she had earned more money than she had ever earned before; and her mother had smiled for the first time since David went out begging, when she poured the halfpence into her lap. Like Euclid she had trudged through the mud of the partially frozen streets for nine or ten miles, besides her walk to the market; and her limbs were weary, and her throat somewhat tired. But her heart was very light. Then the wonderful sight of heaps of money on Euclid's table had dazzled her. Why had they never thought of this trade before? A thousand pities it was; for if they had begun early enough she and David might now have had heaps of money too, like Euclid and Victoria.

Bess was up again before four o'clock in the morning, and was waiting for Euclid when he came downstairs. She was eager to be away, making her fortune. By-and-by Euclid grew used to her company, and liked to hear her talk, as she tripped along by his side. Morning after morning, through darkness and frost, snow and fog, the greyheaded man and the young girl started off on their toilsome tramp; the one with the uncomplaining fortitude of old age, the other with the hopeful courage of youth.

"It 'ill not be such a lonesome shop when I'm gone now, father," said Victoria, one day.

"Why so, Victoria, my dear?" he asked.

"There's Bess," she answered, smiling, but somewhat sadly," you'll take to her, daddy. You two 'ud be two lonesome ones if you didn't take to one another. Mrs. Fell's very near her end, and I am, p'rhaps."

"Do you feel worse, Victoria?" he inquired anxiously.

"Not worse," she said, "but it's so long, the winter is, and there's so much dark, and I lie here, doin' nothin'. If it wasn't for mother's verses and hymns, I don't know what I'd do. I've been sayin' one of 'em all day."

"Which is it, my dear?" he asked.

Victoria's voice fell into a low and solemn tone as she said these words:—

In Prison and Out

> "There is a house, not made with hands,
> Eternal and on high;
> And here my spirit waiting stands,
> Till God shall bid it fly."

"Ay! she were always a sayin' them lines," Euclid murmured softly, "afore you was born, my dear."

"There's enough money to pay for my buryin' now, isn't there, father?" asked Victoria.

"To be sure there is, my dear, lots enough," he answered, "and a bit o' black for Bess, if that 'ill be any comfort to you."

"She's strong, and can help you to get a livin'", observed Victoria, almost joyously, "and there'll be somebody to see as you have a coffin of your own too, daddy. I'm glad to think you'll take to Bess, when I'm gone."

"My work 'ill be done then," said Euclid. "I promised your mother what I'd do, and I've a'most done it. Then I'm ready to go. It's a queer shop this world is!

Chapter 8. THE PRISON CROP ON A YOUNG HEAD

In three calendar months after David Fell was committed to gaol for begging he was released, and sent out again to the old life. He had been regularly supplied with food, kept from the cold of the wintry days and nights, and properly exercised with a careful regard to his health. He had never had three months of so much physical comfort before; and he had grown a good deal both in size and strength. Moreover, he had been diligently taught in school, and could read and write very much better, and with more ease than when he had written his short letter to his mother. He had learned cobbling, and could mend a pair of boots quite creditably. The governor of the gaol enumerated these advantages to him as he gave him a few words of parting counsel.

"Now, my lad," he continued, "don't let me seeyou here again, or hear of you being in trouble elsewhere. This is the second time you've been in gaol—"

In Prison and Out

"Please, sir," interrupted David, with energy, 'I never was in gaol before. It was another boy, not me. I've done nothin' worse than beggin'".

"Don't go away with a lie on your tongue," said the governor sternly; "it's a sad thing to break the laws of your country, but it's worse to break God's laws. 'Thou shalt not steal!' 'Thou shalt not lie!' are His laws. 'Thou shalt not beg,' is your country's law. Keep them in mind and you'll not get into trouble again."

David heard the prison–gate close behind him, leaving him free again in the open streets, with an odd feeling of strangeness and timidity mingled with his delight. The other prisoners, released at the same time, quickly vanished out of sight, as if they did not care to be seen under the gaol walls. But David lingered, half bewildered and half fascinated, gazing up at the strong, grim edifice, with its massive doors, and small, closely barred windows. It had been his home for three months. He was no longer a stranger to it, or its ways. If he should ever come there again, he could fall at once into its customs and rules, and would need very little, if any, instruction from its warders. Just now it seemed more familiar and less formidable to him than the narrow, dirty, squalid street, where his former neighbours lived, and his mother, and little Bess.

He had some miles to go, and it was almost dusk when he reached his own neighbourhood. But though he was stronger and better fitted for labour than when he left it three months ago, he did not turn boldly into the street, whistling some gay tune as he marched along, and calling aloud to this neighbour and that, ready for all sorts of boyish pranks, and equally ready to render little acts of help and kindness to any one who needed them. He waited till night fell, and then went slinking down close to the walls, and keeping as much in the shadow as possible. Blackett's door was open, and he dare not face Blackett. He had always held up his head high above Blackett's sons, except Roger, and he knew both father and sons hated him for it. Did the neighbours know that he had been in prison? If they did not, his closely cropped head, with the hair growing like short fur all over it, would betray him at once.

He stood in a dark corner over against the house, watching its inmates pass to and fro. There was old Euclid going in, with his empty basket; it was quite empty, so he must have had a good day; and presently he saw the glimmer of a candle in the garret window. What would Victoria say, when she saw him, and his prison crop, for the first time? He was almost as much afraid of her and Euclid as he was of Blackett. Could he make them

In Prison and Out

believe that he had only been in gaol for begging? Surely they would not be too hard on him for that! Yet he felt the old glow of shame–again at the thought of going out to beg.

His mother would believe it, and know it to be–true. He was longing for the sight of her, but he dare not go past Blackett's open door. The tears smarted under his eyelids as he thought of how soon now he was going to see her. Then a dark dread crossed his mind. He had been away for three months, and suppose his mother should be dead! Oh! if that could be! Dead and buried, and he never to see her again!

At length Blackett came out, and staggered up the street towards the enticing spirit vaults at the corner. Now was the moment. He crept cautiously to the entrance, and then darted through the lighted passage, almost at a bound. In an instant his hand was on the latch and flinging open his mother's door, he rushed in panting, and closed it after him as if fearful of being pursued. He could hardly see for a moment, though there was a candle in the room. But when he looked round, there was his mother lying on the bare sacking of her miserable bed, her face pale as death, and her sunken eyes, with a famished, ravenous expression in them, fastened eagerly on him. They told a tale of terrible suffering. It seemed to David as if he had almost forgotten his mother's face while he had been in gaol, and that now he saw it afresh, with all the story of her pain and anguish printed upon it. He stood motionless, staring at her; and she lifted herself upon the bed, and held out her arms to him.

"Oh, Davy! my boy! Davy!" she cried, "come–to me! come quickly!"

With a deep groan, such as is rarely wrung from the lips of a man, the boy flung himself into his mother's arms: and the mother bore the shock of agony it caused her without a cry.

This was her son, her first–born. He was the baby who had first lain on her bosom, now so tortured with ceaseless pain, and who had filled her whole heart with love and joy. She could recollect how his father had looked down upon them both, with mingled pride and shyness. She almost forgot her pain in the rapture of fondling him once again. Her shrivelled, wasted hand, whose fingers were drawn up with long years of toil, stroked his poor head, with its prison crop of hair, where the baby's flaxen curls had grown; and her lips were pressed again and again to his face. She could not let him go.

In Prison and Out

"I was doin' nothin' but beg for you, mother," he sobbed out at last.

"I know, Davy, I know," she said, sinking back exhausted, but still holding fast his hand, and devouring him with her eyes, "it couldn't be no sin, God in heaven knows. You'll make a good man yet, in spite of all, like your father, Davy. You're as like him as like can be!"

She lay looking at him with a smile on her face. So much care had been taken of him in the gaol that he looked more like a man, or at least gave more promise of growing into a strong, capable man like his father, than he had ever done whilst he starved on scanty fare at home. His face, too, had lost its boyish carelessness, and wore an air of thought, almost of gloom, such as sits on most men's faces.

"May be I ought to ha' gone into the House," she said, as her eyes caught sight of David's short, dark hair; "it's bad for folks to say you ever went a-beggin', and was took up for it. But I never knew nobody go into the House as I should like to be with, or have Bess be with. Most of the folks as have gone out of our street 'ud shame the bad place itself; and it 'ud be worse than dyin' to live among 'em all day, and all night too. I always said, and I promised father when he was dyin', I swore a oath to him, as long as I could stand at a tub I'd never mix myself up with such a lot, or let his boy and girl go among 'em. But may be I ought to ha' given in instead of lettin' you go a–beggin'", she added, with a profound sigh.

"No, no, mother; don't you fret about me," answered David. "Why! I've learnt a trade in—there," he said, avoiding the name gaol, "and I know how to work now, and I'll keep you and Bess. Sometimes I used to think, s'pose they'd only taught me outside, without goin' inside that place! I'd have learnt it with more heart, and never got the bad name as folks will give me now. I can mend boots and shoes prime; and I can read and write almost like a scholar. But I shall never get over being in there!"

"Oh! you will, you will, my lad," cried his mother, faintly and sadly.

"No, I can't never forget it," he said, with a look of shame and sorrow on his face. "Father's name was always good, and mine never can be. Mother, if they'd only tried to find out if I spoke true! But they didn't take no time or trouble. I didn't know where I was afore the magistrate said, 'Three months!' and they bundled me away, as if I weren't worth taking trouble about. I'm a gaol-bird now."

"No, no," sobbed his mother.

"That's what the neighbours 'ill call me," he went on, "and Blackett 'ill crow over me. They'll never believe I was only beggin'. I feel as if I couldn't hold my head up to face them; or Bess. Where's Bess, mother?"

But as he spoke Bess came in, and with a cry of delight ran to him, and flung her arms round his neck. He could not rid himself of those clinging arms, and he burst into a passion of weeping as Bess kissed him again and again.

"They were wicked, cruel people as sent you to gaol, Davy," she repeated, over and over again, "cruel and wicked; cruel and wicked!"

It was some minutes before they could speak to one another in any other words, or before Bess remembered on what errand she had been absent when David came home.

"They can't let us have the ring this evening, mother," she said, after a while. "Mr. Quirk's away till this time to-morrow; and Mrs. Quirk says as she daren't part with any o' the rings without him."

"What ring?" asked David.

"Mother's ring," answered Bess.

"We were forced to part with it, Davy," said his mother, in a pleading tone, as if to justify herself to him. "I'd clemmed myself till I could bear it no longer, and everything else was gone. It was the last time I set foot out o' doors; I carried it myself to Mr. Quirk's, and swore as I'd redeem it. And Bess there has earned money to redeem it, and we thought we'd get it back to-night. But you're come back instead, my lad; and I can bear to go without the ring."

His mother's wedding-ring had been all his life to him a sacred thing; the only sacred thing he knew of. It was blended with all his earliest childish thoughts of his dead father, whom he had never known, but of whom his mother talked so often of an evening when work was done, and she wore the ring, and when the glimmer of it in the dim fire-light made it visible, though almost all else was in darkness. All the inherent superstition and reverence for sacred symbols common to our nature centred for David in his mother's wedding-ring. He knew what straits of gnawing hunger Bess and his mother must have undergone before they would part with it; and his bitterness and heaviness of heart, for he had left gaol in bitterness and heaviness of heart, were increased tenfold by this loss of her ring.

"We'll have it to-morrow," he said, in a stern and passionate voice.

Yet they were on the whole happy that evening: it was so much to be together again. Bess had plenty to tell of her daily tramps through the streets; and David talked of his plans for the future; whilst their mother listened to them, thankful beyond all words to have her boy in her sight once more. Even during the night, when she heard him turning uneasily to and fro on the scanty heap of straw they had managed to get for him to lie on, so hard to him after his comfortable hammock and warm rug in the gaol, her heart felt lighter than it had done for many months. Her poverty continued, her sore pain was not less agonising; but David was at home again, and life was once more dear to her.

Chapter 9. BROKEN-HEARTED

Bess was up as usual in the morning, and David would have gone with her but for Euclid. He shrank from meeting any of the neighbours; and if it had been possible he would have remained in-doors till his hair had grown long again. All the day he stayed in the dark, unwholesome room, talking at times with his mother, but generally sitting silent, with his head resting on his hands. The hours seemed endless. Hunger and cold he had borne with courage, and he could do so still; but shame he could not bear. Pride in a good name was the only moral lesson he had been taught; and his good name was gone. His mother had sympathy enough to guess what troubled him, but she did not know how to comfort him. There was a vague indistinct feeling in their minds that he had not forfeited his good name—he had been robbed of it.

At last evening came, and Bess went out again to redeem the precious pledge. Both David and his mother forgot their troubles for a brief space of time as they thought of seeing it shine once more on her hand, so wasted and shrivelled now, and different from

In Prison and Out

the firm young hand that had first worn it. It had been a brand new ring when David Fell bought it—no other would satisfy the proud young artisan—a thick, heavy ring of gold, such as the finest lady in the land might wear.

"It's here, mother!" cried Bess, running in almost breathless, with the small, precious packet in her hand. David lighted the candle, and held it beside his mother, as her trembling fingers unfolded the paper in which it was wrapped. But what was this? A thin, battered ring, worn almost to a thread. No more like the one they all knew so well, than this bare and desolate room was like the pleasant house David Fell had provided for his young wife. Mrs. Fell uttered a bitter cry of disappointment and dread.

"Oh, Davy," she cried, "it isn't mine! it isn't mine!"

In two minutes from that fatal cry of despair, David, panting, bare-headed, nearly mad with passion, stood on the pavement in front of the pawnshop. There was no need to enter it, for Mr. Quirk was pacing to and fro in front of hIs premises, inviting the passer-by to inspect his goods. He was a short, undersized, knavish-looking man. David confronted him with a white face and dilating nostrils, holding out the ring to him.

"It is'nt mother's," he gasped; "you've given Bess somebody else's ring. This ain't mother's ring."

"That's Mary Fell's ring," drawled Mr. Quirk sneeringly, and as coolly as if he had prepared himself for the charge, "as she pledged here to me, two months ago. That's her ring."

"Give me my mother's own ring!" shouted David, every nerve and muscle tingling with all the force and energy he had in him, "give me her ring, you swindling thief!"

"It's Mary Fell's ring," repeated the pawnbroker stubbornly, "and Mary Fell's well known as a thief and a drunkard, and something worse!

Scarcely had the words against his mother's good name been pronounced, before David had flung himself, in his rage and the unusual vigour he had brought from gaol, upon the puny man, who was unprepared for the attack. The boy and the man were not ill-matched, and blow after blow was given. The battered old ring fell to the pavement, and was trodden under their feet. A circle of spectators gathered as if by magic about them in an instant, none of whom cared to interrupt the sport such a contest afforded. There were cries and cheers of encouragement on all hands, until the combatants fell, David uppermost.

"What's all this about?" inquired a policeman, elbowing his way through the crowd, and calmly looking on for a minute, whilst David still struck hard at his enemy, who was struggling up to his feet. The policeman seized the lad by the collar, and he tried to shake off his hold, as he faced the pawnbroker, blind and deaf with rage.

"Give me my mother's ring!" he shouted.

"I give him in charge," said Mr. Quirk, welcoming the policeman's interference; whilst David felt an awful thrill of despair run through him as he saw whose hand was grasping him. "I was a–doin' nothin', and he up at me like a tiger," added the pawnbroker.

"Ay, he did; I saw him," cried a woman, standing at the pawnshop door; "he's a young gaol–bird; everybody can see that."

It was only too plainly to be seen. David was now standing perfectly still in the policeman's grip—pale and frightened, with a hang–dog air, which told powerfully against him. One of the passers–by, an intelligent, well–dressed mechanic, pressed forward a little, asking, "Why did you meddle with the man? What's this about a ring?" But the policeman checked David's attempts to reply.

"That's no business of mine," he said sharply; "you give this lad in charge?"

He addressed himself to Mr. Quirk, who replied plaintively—"I'm a householder and a ratepayer," he said, "and I give him in charge."

"Then you'll make your defence before the Court," said the policeman to David. "Come along with you!"

David glanced round the cluster of faces hemming him in. Some of them he knew. Blackett was there, grinning triumphantly, and Roger was peeping behind him, half afraid of being caught by his father. Euclid had stopped for a moment, with his basket on his

In Prison and Out

arm, and was looking on with an amazed and puzzled face. David dared not call upon any of them by name, but he cried out, in a lamentable voice which touched and startled many of the careless on-lookers,

"Will somebody tell my mother what's befell me?"

He saw Roger make him a sign that he had heard and would fulfil his request, before he was marched off to the police-station, to pass a night there—no longer a strange and unprecedented occurrence to David.

Bess had set the door of their room a little ajar, and was waiting anxiously for David's return. Her mother had not ceased to sob over her lost ring from the moment when she had caught sight of the worn-out, battered thing which had been exchanged for her own. Her grief was the more keen as she had little hope of David recovering the right one. She had heard of other women having their wedding-rings changed or "sweated," and never being able to right themselves, and she could not bear to think of some other woman, happier than herself, wearing it as her wedding-ring, and prizing it as she had done. A thousand dim memories and inarticulate thoughts centred in the lost ring, none the less real, perhaps, because the poor widow was only an ignorant woman, and could not express her feelings in language. She lay moaning in utter hopelessness and helplessness, knowing too well it was lost for ever. Before even they could expect David back, Roger ran in, breathless and stammering. The candle was still burning, and they could see his agitated face and his excited gestures plainly.

"He's bein' took to gaol again!" he exclaimed, in broken sentences. "I see him all along. He up and at old Quirk as brave as a bulldog. He had him down on the ground in no time. He'd said as you was a thief, and a drunkard, and worse; and David couldn't stand it. I'd ha' had a cut at him too, but he had him down on his back in a moment's time; and he fought for you like a good un!"

"But where is he?" gasped the mother, as her eyes, glistening with terror, turned towards the door, where Bess was standing, as though waiting to let David in and close it safely after him.

"He's took to gaol, you know," answered Roger, 'with an oath such as he had learned when he could first speak. "There was a bobby up afore I could give him warnin', pushin' through everybody; and old Quirk gave him in charge, and they walked him off to the station, to be shut up all night till to-morrow mornin'. And he shouted, 'Somebody tell my mother what's befell me!' And he looked straight at me, and I came off at wunst. Perhaps they'll let him go free in the mornin'!"

But even Roger's unaccustomed eyes could see the deathlike pallor and change that came over the face of David's mother, as she heard what he had to say. She uttered no word or cry, but sank down again on her miserable death-bed, and turned her despairing face to the wall. Bess sent away Roger, and carefully putting out the candle, crept on to the sacking beside her, and laying her arm gently across her, spoke hopefully of David being released, and Quirk punished, as soon as the truth was known. But Mrs. Fell was at last broken-hearted, and answered not a word, even to little Bess, who fell asleep at last, crying softly to herself.

Who can tell how long the hours of that night were? Darkness without, and within the utter blackness of despair. The craving hunger of disease, and the soul's hunger after the welfare of her children! The chilly dew of death, and the icy death-blow dealt to every lingering hope for them! When Bess awoke and bestirred herself early in the morning, her mother still lay speechless, and she dared not leave her. Euclid started on his day's work alone. There was no one she could ask for help; so she set about her little tasks of lighting a handful of fire, and making a cup of tea for her mother, which she could not persuade her to touch. It was a dark and dreary winter's morning; so dark where she was living that she could scarcely see her mother's face.

The afternoon was fast fading into night, another night of misery and despair, when Roger stole softly in and crept gently up to the side of the bed where David's mother lay. Bess was sitting by her, holding her hand closely, as if she could thus keep her in the world where her lot had been so hard. She had not spoken yet, and had scarcely moved since Roger had brought his fatal tidings the night before. Now when her ear caught the sound of his low, awe-struck voice, she opened her eyes once more, and fastened them upon him. He stooped down and spoke to her in a sorrowful whisper.

"He's got three months agen," he said. "Never mind! everybody gets into gaol some time o' their lives!

Mrs. Fell's lips moved tremulously, as the eyelids closed slowly over her dim eyes, which were losing sight of Bess, though she was leaning over her and calling "Mother!"

"He might ha' been a good man like his father! she moaned, with her dying breath.

Chapter 10. BLACKETT'S THREATS

A parish coffin and a pauper's grave were all the country had to give to the dead mother, whose son, in the ignorance and recklessness of boyhood, had broken the laws twice, and been each time visited with a harsh penalty. "That servant which knew his lord's will and did it not, shall be beaten with many stripes. But he that knew not, and did commit things worthy of stripes, shall be beaten with few stripes." There is Christ's rule. Do we, who sometimes pride ourselves as being the most Christian nation on the face of the earth, abide by that rule?

The mother was buried; and what was to become of Bess? No one was bound to take any care of her. She was old enough to see after herself. There was the workhouse open to her, if she chose to apply for admission; but if she entered it, it would be to be sent out to service as a workhouse girl, in the course of a few weeks or months, untrained and untaught, fit only for the miserable drudgery of the lowest service. There was not strength enough in her slight ill-fed frame to enable her to keep body and soul together at laundry-work, which was the only work she knew anything of. There was no home, however wretched, to give her shelter, if she continued to sell water-cresses in the streets. True, Blackett offered the refuge of his lodgings, and Roger urged her eagerly to avail herself of his father's kindness; but Bess shrank away with terror from the mere thought of it. Blackett had been the object of her daily dread ever since her childhood, and no change in him could inspire her with confidence.

When she came back from following her mother's coffin to its pauper's grave she stole past Blackett's door into the empty room beyond, and sat down, worn out with grief and weariness, on the bedstead where her mother's corpse had been lying for the last three days. She had lived in the room alone with it, and she felt more lonely now that it was gone. Silent and motionless as it had been, with its half-closed eyelids, and the ashy whiteness of its face gleaming even in the dusk, it had been a companion to her, and she had not been afraid of it. Now it was gone, she was, indeed, alone.

In Prison and Out

There was not a single article of furniture left in the room, except this low, rough, pallet bedstead, with the dingy sacking, bare of bed and bed-clothes. Everything else was gone. There was now no candlestick left, no tea-pot or cup, no flat-iron or poker; not one of the small household goods of the very poor. Bess had carried all the few possessions left to her, in a miscellaneous lot, to get what she could for them, at the marine stores. She would have carried off the bedsteads if they had not been too heavy for her; or if her mother's corpse had not been lying there.

Euclid, her only friend, had not been near her these three days. The truth is that the poor old man was passing through a great and severe struggle, and it was not over yet. He had grown in a measure fond of Bess, and his heart was grieved to the very core for her. But what was he to do? he continually asked himself. What could a poor old man like him do? He was terribly afraid of taking any additional weight upon his overburdened shoulders, especially now he was in sight of his goal. For the last year or two, as he felt the infirmities of age growing heavier, an unspeakable dread lodged in his inmost soul, lest, after all, he should fail in his life's aim. Could he endure to see Victoria buried as Mrs. Fell was? He had lurked in a dark corner of the staircase, and watched the rough and reckless way in which the rude, slight box, that could hardly be called a coffin, was bundled out of the house, and carried off along the street, followed by Bess alone, as the only mourner for the dead. It had given a sharp and poignant prick to his hidden fears. How could he burden himself with the care of Bess while there was any chance of such an ending to his career, or worse still, to Victoria's? If Victoria had been buried in her own coffin, as his wife, and the other children had been, he might have taken up with Bess. But she seemed no nearer the grave than at the beginning of the winter: her health, or rather her complaint, whatever it was, remained stationary. No; he must not sacrifice Victoria to Bess.

Poor Bess! But as she was sitting alone in the gathering twilight, bewildered with her sorrow, she heard the door softly opened, and as softly closed again. It was Victoria who had come in, after crawling feebly down the long flights of stairs, which she had mounted four months ago, in the autumn, for the last time as she thought. She could not speak yet, and she sat down breathless and silent beside the desolate girl. There was a mournful stillness as of death in the room, though all around were echoing the busy, jarring noises of common life.

In Prison and Out

"I don't know much," said Victoria at last in her low, weak voice, "but I've dreams sometimes, lyin' up there alone all day, and I seem to see quite plain some place where the sun is always shinin', and folks are happy, and there mother is! I saw it last night, betwixt sleepin' and wakin', as plain as I see you, and your mother was there, Bess; and some one, I couldn't see His face, was leadin' her to where the sun was warm and bright, and choosin' a good place for her to rest in; and He looked as if He was watchin' for any little bit o' stone in the way for fear she'd hurt her feet, like we might do wi' a little, little child, just learnin' to go alone. And, oh! Bess, your mother turned so as I could see her face and it was very pale, but very peaceful. There wasn't any more pain in it."

"Is it true?" sobbed Bess.

"I don't know much," repeated Victoria. "I never went to school, for father couldn't pay for my schoolin'; and there wasn't any law to make him. He'd have done it gladly, but water-cresses isn't much for a family to live on. But I think it must be true, or how could I see it? I told father what I'm tellin' you; and I said to him 'Father, it don't matter very much about bein' buried in our own coffins, if we get to a place like that after all.'"

"And what did he say?" asked Bess.

"He made a noise like 'Umph!' and went off," answered Victoria.

"If there was only somebody to tell us true!" sobbed Bess again.

"Father won't let the missioners come to see me," went on Victoria; "he says they teaches cants to get coals, and he'd as soon get his coals from the parish. There was a sister o' mother's as was converted, and they put her into what they call a Report, and father was that ashamed! None on us had ever been in such a thing. We never had nothing to do with her, so as I don't know if it's true. Father says as he likes to see religion, and he don't see nothink he could call religion in her, or in most folks as are converted and put in the Report. I never knew rightly what converted means," said Victoria, sighing sadly, and speaking in a low voice, as if to herself.

But Bess was thinking no longer of Victoria's dreams. Her thoughts had gone in again, brooding over their own sorrows, and she moaned with a very deep and bitter moaning.

In Prison and Out

"Oh! what shall I do?" she cried, "what shall I do?"

"I came to fetch you up-stairs to live with us," answered Victoria, very softly; "father 'ill be glad enough when it's done. You'd be as good as another daughter to father if I was gone; and nobody knows how soon that may be. He's a bit shy and queer just now, but that'll be gone when it's all settled. You shall help me up-stairs again, Bess; and when father comes he'll get somebody to help him carry these bedsteads up for you and me to sleep on. It'll be better for me than sleepin' on the floor, you know."

When Euclid reached home an hour later, he paused before going up-stairs, and knocked at the door of Mrs. Fell's room; but there was no answer. He tried to open it, but it was locked. Where could little Bess be? he asked himself in sudden terror. She must be come back from the funeral by this time. Was it possible that she had taken shelter with Blackett? The old man's withered face tingled, and his frame shook as with ague, when the thought flashed across him. Whose fault would it be? It was he who had forsaken Bess in her misery; the fatherless, motherless, brotherless girl. He stood outside the closed and locked door, thinking of her light footstep and pretty face, tripping along at his side every morning for the last two months. He had not known how close she had crept to his heart until now the dread was beating against him that she was gone to Blackett! The old man's grey and grim face grew greyer and grimmer. It would be a hard thing, no doubt, to follow Victoria to the grave in a pauper's coffin; but, oh! it would be even harder to see Bess flaunting about the streets, a lost and wretched creature. His conscience smote him sharply. And now what must he do? What did he dare to do? It would be like braving a lion in his den to face Blackett at his own fireside. Yet probably Bess was there!

"God help this old tongue o' mine!" said Euclid, half aloud, as after some minutes of hesitation, he turned with desperate courage to knock at Blackett's door.

"Come in;" shouted Blackett, with a surly snarl.

Euclid opened the door, and stood humbly on the threshold. It was a room less bare, but more squalid with dirt than any other in the house. The woman who had been the mother of Blackett's three sons, had long ago disappeared; and what little cleanliness and comfort had once been known there had gone with her. The air was stifling with the fumes of tobacco and spirits, and Blackett was smoking over a fireplace choked up with ashes.

In Prison and Out

Roger, who was bound hand and foot with strong cords, had rolled himself out of reach of his fathers's kicks, and was lying in a corner with an expression of terror and hatred on his face. But Bess was nowhere to be seen.

"Come in and shut the door!" shouted Blackett.

"Mr. Blackett," said Euclid, shutting the door behind him, with the long-sleeping courage of manhood stirring in his old heart, "have you seen aught of Mrs. Fell's little Bess?"

"Ay, have I!" growled Blackett with an oath. "Victoria's been and fetched her up to your rat-hole; and now I give you fair warning, old fellow, if you go to harbour that girl, I'll make this place too hot for you. I'll keep a eye on you going out and coming in, and you'll repent it sore. Get out o' this like a shot, or I'll begin on it at once."

But Euclid was off like a shot, before Blackett had finished his threats, and was mounting to his garret with a suddenly gladdened heart. "Thank God! thank God!" he repeated to himself, step after step up the long staircase. He had hardly heeded Blackett's menaces, though they lodged themselves unconsciously in his mind, and came back to his memory when his first gladness was over. Bess had fallen asleep for sorrow on Victoria's bed, and he stooped over her and laid his hard brown hand gently on her head, as if to welcome her to her new home. "God bless her!" he murmured.

Chapter 11. AN UNWILLING THIEF

Blackett's hatred and vengeance were no mean forces which Euclid could afford to forget or disregard. His enemy had him at an advantage, inasmuch as he could neither go in nor out of the house without passing the door of his room, where he might be lurking in ambush against him. Euclid was a peaceable, inoffensive old man, who had kept himself aloof from his neighbours in dread of falling into disturbances. It worried him to feel that he had made such a man his eneny, and at times he reflected on the possibility of moving; but Victoria's ill-health and weakness seemed to make that impossible, even if he could find an equally cheap attic in the neighbourhood.

In Prison and Out

He did not know it, nor did Victoria, but for some time past a rumour had pervaded the house that old Euclid the water-cress seller was a miser, a miser also of the old-fashioned type, who kept his money in hard cash, and in his own hands. Some of his neighbours said he carried untold wealth about with him in the old waistcoat which he always wore, summer and winter, under his linen blouse. Others guessed that every chink and crevice in the walls of his garret contained bank notes and coins, and that Victoria's constant ill-health was nothing but a blind to account for her never leaving the treasure unguarded. Both Euclid and Victoria became the objects of unusual attention, and Victoria, especially, was surprised and embarrassed by the friendly visits of the neighbours during her father's absence in the day-time, who came to offer her any assistance she needed. But Victoria was now quite independent. Bess made the bed and scrubbed the floor, and did the little shopping that had to be done, and the sick girl had never been so comfortable and cared for in her life.

No doubt it was Bess herself who had innocently set these rumours afloat. No one can tell whether she had hinted at it in any confidential talk with Roger, or whether some prying neighbour, listening in the common entrance, had overheard her telling her mother of the wonderful sight she had beheld through the chink in old Euclid's door. Bess was too busy to hear anything of these whispered reports, and they were not likely to reach the ears of Euclid and Victoria. Neither of these ever spoke of their treasure in the presence of Bess, and Victoria always carefully removed it from under her pillow before Bess made the bed. It had not grown at all since Mrs. Fell's funeral day; nay, once it had been broken into to pay the rent. Yet neither of them repented befriending Bess.

One consequence of Bess living up in the garret was, that it became a not unusual circumstance for Roger Blackett to mount up there, partly for her sake and partly to seek a refuge from his father's cruel tyranny. Blackett knew it very well, but, with a crafty foresight that this might be useful some day, feigned an utter ignorance of this new intercourse. Roger seldom showed his face when Euclid was at home; but Victoria soon grew used to see him creep in timidly, with his terrified, downcast face, and crouch on the hearth before the handful of fire, showing her the bruises on his arms and shoulders and back, where his father had been flogging him. He was an idler, weaker boy than David Fell, with little energy to swim against the tide of evil that was ready to sweep him away in its current. But as yet he had never fallen into the hands of the police, and now he promised Victoria, as he had been wont to promise Mrs. Fell, that he would always be a good boy, and keep from being a thief.

In Prison and Out

To Victoria it was pleasant to have this fresh young life of Bess and Roger coming about her, to divert the dreary solitude of her illness. Hitherto she had had no companionship except that of an old man borne down by cares, and Euclid was amazed to find how cheerful she grew, and how much less the winter was trying her than he had feared. But the change, though he did not grudge Bess her home, was not so welcome to him as to Victoria. The mere fact that he could never speak of his own aim in life before Bess, nor count over his hoard as he had been used to do, made him more anxious about it, and he could not get the thought of it out of his head while he was away all day, crying his cresses in the distant streets.

"Victoria, my dear," he said one evening when he was home before Bess, and had treated himself to a hasty and furtive glance at his treasure, "I'm castin' about in my mind if we couldn't find a safer place for it, now we've so many strange folks about us. If I only knew somebody as 'ud take good care on it for us!"

"It's never from under my pillow, father," answered Victoria with a smile; "it's as safe as safe can be. Don't you fidget, daddy."

"If I could only lock the door when we go out i' th' mornin'!" sighed old Euclid.

"And leave me locked up all day!" said Victoria, laughing.

"Bess has been with us four weeks," he went on, "and we haven't put a penny to it! And Blackett gives me a curse every time he catches sight on me!"

"Father," she said earnestly, "I'd ten times rather be buried in a parish coffin than turn Bess away into the streets."

"Ay! so would I for myself, lass," he answered, "but it 'ud be hard work to me to follow thee in a parish coffin!"

It was still as dark as midnight at four o'clock the next morning when Euclid and Bess, after giving Victoria a cup of tea, left her to sleep away the remainder of the night until daybreak. Her best and soundest sleep generally came to her after they were gone, when she was alone in the quiet garret, past which no foot could tramp, and above which was the roof inhabited only by the sparrows.

In Prison and Out

If Euclid and Bess could have looked through the panels of Blackett's door as they passed it, they would have seen that he was up, and listening; and that Roger was cowering behind him with a scared and haggard expression on his wretched face. In about a quarter of an hour after their departure Roger was being pushed on by his father, with smothered threats and curses in his ears, up the dark staircase, and past the doors of the rooms, whose inmates would be all astir in another hour or less. Roger crept slowly and reluctantly up the last steep flight, and lingered a moment at Euclid's door, while Blackett stood half-way below him, a black figure in the deep gloom, beckoning to him with a threatening gesture to go onwards.

Roger pushed the latchless door gently, and found that it was not fastened within, but yielded at once to his touch. The small fire of coals and wood lit by Bess had smouldered down, and showed only a line of red between the two lowest bars, yet the faint light it gave fell upon the pale face of Victoria already sleeping a quiet and restful slumber. He looked from that pale, sleeping face back to the tall black figure in the darkness, with its uplifted and clenched fist menacing him, and he trode noiselessly into the room. Still he paused for some minutes, dreading to go on, though not daring to go back. Victoria was kind and good to him; but his father was threatening to kill him if he did not execute his commands. Why had he ever learned that old Euclid was a miser, and had heaps of money? and oh! how could it be that he had ever betrayed to his father the secret he had found out, that Victoria guarded some precious bundle under her pillow? If he must be a thief, he would a thousand times rather steal from any one than her.

A very slight, but to Roger a very terrible sound, upon the staircase, filled him with a sudden courage. He stretched himself on the floor, and crawled forward to Victoria's side. Very warily and softly his fingers stole up, and under her pillow, where the precious bundle lay. He drew it so slowly and gently towards him that though Victoria moved a little restlessly, and put her hand up sleepily as if to guard it, she did not wake. In a few moments it lay in his grasp, and he was crawling back across the floor to the dark staircase. The door creaked a little on its rusty hinges as he closed it after him, and he heard Victoria's voice calling out drowsily, "Good-bye, father!"

It was after mid-day before Victoria got up; for she was neither so hungry nor so cold in bed, and it saved firing to lie still as long as she could bear to do so. She had asked Roger the day before to come up for some pence to buy chips and coal, and he had promised readily to do it, but he never came. She had just chips enough to kindle the fire, and sufficient coal to keep it alight till Bess or her father should come home. But she could not help wondering what cruelty of his father's was keeping him away, as she watched the tiny tongues of flame, which had to be carefully cherished lest they should die out altogether before the coal was lit. She felt hopeful and happy. The late February days were come, and the sky was clearer; the dense fogs had almost gone for another spell of brighter weather, and the clouds that still hung grey above the streets had gleams of blue breaking through them. The deepest misery of the year was over. The days were longer, and would soon be warmer; there was no dreary mid-winter to tide over. Victoria, watching her small fire, not quite kindled yet, sang feebly to herself in a piping, tremulous voice, and her wan face wore a brighter smile than it had done for months.

"Why! there's father comin' up the stairs," she exclaimed; "he's more than an hour early!"

It was Euclid who came in with an empty basket and a pleased face. He had had uncommon good luck, he said, as he sat down before the fire, and stretched his wrinkled old hands over the flame and smoke. He had been reckoning up as he came along home, and he could spare seven-pence half-penny to add to the hoard, and so make it level money. Euclid was always uneasy in his mind when his deposit was not level money. Now Bess was away, and sure to be away for another hour or more, he could count the money over, and feast his eyes upon it: the only pleasure he had in the world.

"It does my old heart good, Victoria, my dear," he said, turning up the old soap-box on end; "it's as if it made up for all the pipes I never smoke, and the victuals I never eat, and the sights as I never see. Make the door fast, my dear, and you and me'll have a treat."

Victoria fastened the door with a forked stick, brought from the market, laughing a low, quiet laugh, in which Euclid joined hoarsely yet heartily. It was as great a treat to him to hear her laugh as to count up his money.

"I've heard a learned man, a great scholar he was," said Euclid, "as had read a heap o' books, talk o' bein' as rich as creases; but whatever be could ha' meant by it, I could never make out yet.

I've puzzled over it many and many a hour. If be'd said as cold as creases, or yet as green as creases, I could ha' understood. But as rich as creases, Victoria, my dear!"

In Prison and Out

"Don't ask me, father," she answered, "I'm no scholar. We've lived on creases, but we've never got rich on 'em."

"Ay, we've lived and died on 'em," said Euclid, contemplatively. "If we could have all the money as ever we spent, all that's gone in rent, and victuals, and clothin' and ceterer, we might, may be, ha' grown rich by creases; but then where should we ha' been?"

Victoria had lifted up her pillow, as he spoke half to himself and half to her. She stood for an instant gazing down in bewilderment. The old cotton handkerchief, once white with a red border round it, but grown yellow and dingy with age, and with much knotting and unknotting; the familiar little bundle that had been her father's purse ever since she could remember, did not lie in its accustomed place. She pushed aside the parcel of rags which served Bess as a pillow, but it was not there. She shook the clothes with a trembling hand, and then sank down on the bedstead, sick and faint with alarm.

"Father!" she breathed in a low, gasping voice, "it's gone!"

For a moment old Euclid gazed at her in a dreamy, absent manner, muttering "As rich as creases!" as though he did not hear her speak.

"Father!" she cried again, in a louder tone, "Our money's gone!"

"Gone!" he repeated.

"It's not here!" she answered, "it's been stolen! stolen! I remember now. There was a click of the door, after I'd fallen asleep, and I called out 'Good–bye, father!' and it was a thief! Oh, father! father! what shall we do?"

Euclid had started to his feet, and stood trembling and shivering with the shock of terror. Gone! Stolen! The little hoard of money he had scraped together, with so many hardships and cares, so much labour and self–denial! The money he might want before the bleak winds of March were gone to bury his last child in her own coffin! Was it possible that God would allow a thief to steal in, and rob him of such a sacred treasure? Euclid's heart answered yes, it was possible, it had come to pass, this overwhelming disaster, and his very soul seemed to die within him.

In Prison and Out

He sat down again in his broken old chair, for he felt too feeble to hold himself up, and he hid his withered, ashy-pale face in his hands. All the misery, and privation, and pinching poverty of his sixty years of life seemed to rush back upon him, and roll like a full tide over his crushed spirit. After all his toil and suffering he would be forced to go upon the parish, if not to-day or this week, well! in a few weeks, or in a few months at the farthest. He might as well give up at once, for he could never save so much money again. And Victoria! Now, if she should fall ill, even a little worse, she must be taken away from him, and go into the workhouse hospital, to die there, among strange bad women, uncared for, weeping her last bitter tears on a parish pillow! Whilst he, parted from her, was perhaps laying his old grey head on another parish pillow, and turning his face to the wall, to hide his bitter tears.

"I must stir up," he said at last, rising stiffly and slowly from his chair, as if he felt himself to be a very old, infirm man, "I must fetch the police, Victoria."

It was not long before a policeman mounted up to Euclid's garret, and heard the whole story of the loss. Nor was it very long, after inquiring who visited them the oftenest, and after seeking a little information among the neighbours, who very eagerly supplied it, before he fixed upon Roger and his father, as bearing the worst character in the house. Before an hour had passed Roger was lodged in the nearest police-station, and Blackett was being sought for in all his usual places of resort.

Chapter 12. VICTORIA'S COFFIN

But Blacket was nowhere to be found. He had taken his glazier's tools, and a sheet or two of glass on his back, and gone away into the country to seek for stray jobs in the shape of broken panes. There was no trace of the lost money in his room; and though Roger, in his fright, had owned to having stolen it, and added that he had given the whole of it to his father, there was no evidence to prove the truth of his assertion. Roger's terrified statements were full of contradictions and falsehoods. He was ready to assert or deny anything, and he was remanded until his father could be found and summoned; whilst Euclid and Victoria were bidden to hold themselves in readiness to appear, whenever their evidence should be wanted.

In Prison and Out

For the next few days, Euclid, a broken-spirited, hopeless old man, dragged his heavy feet over his old rounds, crying "Cre-she! cre-she!" mournfully, as if by some cruel magic a spell had been cast over him, and he was doomed to tread the dreary streets with bowed-down head and dragging limbs, uttering no other word but "Cre-she!" His eyes discerned nothing save Victoria being carried before him in a parish coffin. He did not even see Blackett on the evening of his return from his expedition in search of work, after a week's absence, who was lying in wait to watch him come home, and jeered after him as he shambled along the passage and up the stairs.

It had been a hard day's work for Euclid, and he was long behind his time. Bess and Victoria had been looking out for him anxiously the last hour or more: and they made much of him, as if they could not do enough to comfort him. But he sat silent and downcast, and only shook his shaggy grey head despondently when Victoria gave him a cup of tea.

"Daddy!" she said, "what's ailin' you?"

"You know, Victoria!" he answered, sadly and reproachfully. "God hasn't helped my poor old legs to keep you and me off the parish. Your poor mother when she lay a-dyin', with you on her poor arm, she said as she were sure He'd do as much as that; and He hasn't."

"Have you been to ask help of the parish?" inquired Bess, with eyes round with wonder and alarm.

"No, no, child, not yet!" he replied, a tinge of brownish red creeping over his grim yet pale face; "it's not come to that as yet. But as I came down the street here in the dusk, there walked alongside of me a parish funeral; not a real funeral, only the shadow of one, as you may say; and I knowed it were Victoria's. It were Victoria's!" he repeated, his voice breaking down into a sob.

"Father!" cried Victoria, "daddy! how do you know as I shall want a funeral or a coffin?"

Euclid lifted up his head, and checked his sobs, gazing at the only child left to him, with his dim old eyes half blinded with tears.

In Prison and Out

"I've been thinking" she went on, "as we've been almost making believe as if I must want a coffin o' my own very soon. May be God hasn't let us keep that money, because He doesn't mean me to die just yet. I've been thinkin' hard ever since it was stole; and that's what's come into my head, father. Perhaps God knows I shan't want a coffin o' my own yet; and there was some harm, may be, in our settin' our minds on it."

"Not want a coffin!" repeated Euclid incredulously.

"No," she said with a faint smile. "I think the thought of it has helped to make me ill. I could go to the Court after the money was stole, and I were none the worse for it; and the p'leece has been here to bid us go again to-morrow, and I feel quite sharp and stirred up like. And I've slept sounder since the money's been gone away from under my head. It was always sayin' quietly in my ear, 'I'm goin' to buy you a coffin! I'm a-goin' to buy a coffin for you!' And then I'd dream of my funeral, and you being left all alone, father. No, God doesn't mean me to want a coffin yet, I think."

Old Euclid sat motionless and speechless, his bowed head lifted up, and his hands firmly grasping his knees, as he gazed fixedly at his daughter. She was very pale, very thin, a small, delicate, weakly creature, but her eyes were brighter, and her face happier than he had seen them since she was a little untroubled child, not old enough to understand his difficulties and toil. The tears started to her eyes for a moment as she met his gaze, but she laughed and nodded to him as she wiped them away. If God meant to leave him Victoria he would not fret about her coffin.

His sleep was disturbed that night, but the waking thoughts that dove it away were happy ones. Had he thought himself an old worn-out man a few hours before Why! there were years of work in him yet, and he would start afresh after to-morrow. If he could only lay by two-pence a day—one shilling a week—for the next two years, that would more than restore his lost treasure. But it should never lie under Victoria's pillow again to sing that dismal song into her ear. He must find a banker for it; and it should grow without her knowledge. Then his heart softened towards Roger, poor lad! What could he do with such a father? One of his own boys had died about his age; and he thought with peaceful regret of him, blending the two lads together in his half-waking, half-dreamy thoughts.

Bess had to start of for the market alone the next morning, leaving Euclid to go to the police-court to appear against Roger. He and Victoria set out in good time, and had to

In Prison and Out

wait a long while in the large entrance–court of it, whilst a squalid and rough crowd of men, women, and children gathered together. Victoria, in her long seclusion in her garret, had beet kept very much apart from her neighbours, and the brutal faces and rough, coarse manners of this crowd frightened her. She was glad when an officer summoned her and her father into the Court.

They bad been there before, yet still the place looked vast and imposing to them, though it was but a small and dimly lighted hall. There were about fifty spectators in it, standing in a small space at the back, looking on and listening in almost unbroken silence. Roger stood at the bar, opposite the magistrate, looking miserable and bewildered. Blackett, dressed decently like a thoroughly respectable workman, glanced towards him from time to time with a glance that made him shiver. Euclid and Victoria gave their evidence again; and the policeman who had arrested Roger told what he had said in admission of the theft. There was no doubt of his guilt, but was his father an accomplice?

There might be a strong suspicion of it in every mind, but there was no proof. Blackett told the magistrate that Roger was a confirmed liar, as well as a confirmed thief. He had often beaten him for his bad conduct, and done his utmost to correct him. He himself had been so hard up for money on the day of the robbery that he had been compelled to go out and seek work through the country. Not a shilling or a penny could be traced to him; and if the lad swore he had given it all to him it was only one out of a thousand lies. He would be glad to have him sent to prison, where he would be taken care of and taught a trade.

"I've got somethin' more to say," exclaimed Euclid, stepping briskly into the witness–box as soon as Blackett quitted it.

He stood in it as if it had been a kind of pulpit, and he a rugged, unkempt, grim old preacher. His ragged grey hair fell over his wrinkled forehead almost to the shaggy eyebrows, under which his dim and faded eyes gleamed again for a few minutes with his earnestness and resolution. He grasped the woodwork before him with both his hands, and turned his gaze alternately from the magistrate to Roger.

"Don't you send him to gaol, my worship," he exclaimed in a tone of fervent entreaty. "I forgive him free, and Victoria forgives him. It were the money for her coffin he stole; and it's come to her mind as God doesn't mean to let her die yet. I was afeard the parish 'ud

In Prison and Out

have to bury her. The parish!" he cried in a shriller voice, which rang through the court. "I was afeard of that, or I'd never ha' gone for the police, never! He's only a young, little lad, my worship; and if you send him to gaol he'll grow up a thief. His two brothers have been in gaol, and they're both thieves for good now. I can't call 'em gaol-birds, they're gaol-chickens, my worship. Oh, my worship! try summat else with Roger. Try what keepin' him out o' gaol 'll do, for it's done no good to his brothers. It makes my heart sore to think as Victoria and me should ha' helped at makin' him a thief. Gaol's no good for young lads; no good at all. I'm a old man, and I've seen enough of it. If you'll only let him go free, my good worship, I'll forgive him, and Victoria forgives him. Only let us never sit at home o' nights, and think as he's been sent to gaol, and made a thief by her and me."

Euclid had spoken rapidly and eagerly, utterly disregarding the somewhat feeble efforts of the nearest policeman to silence him. All who were in the Court listened, as men always listen to urgent, warm-hearted pleading. Victoria's sad and wan little face, turned towards Roger, pleaded for him eloquently, and the boy dropping his face into his hands, broke out into a loud cry as Euclid finished speaking. A gentleman who was sitting on a seat behind the officials of the Court, wrote a few words hurriedly on a slip of paper, and had it passed to the magistrate, who glanced at it, and then turned to Euclid.

"At your request," he said, "I shall not pass sentence on this lad to-day, but remand him for another week. Some inquiries shall be made into Blackett's circumstances and means of helping to pay for the maintenance of his son, and also if any industrial school is open to take him. Blackett, if your two elder sons are thieves, it speaks very badly for you, and I shall direct the police to keep an eye upon you and your movements. You may go now."

There was an ominous scowl of hatred on Blackett's face as he crushed passed Euclid and Victoria on their way out. Euclid caught sight of it, but he did not speak of it to Victoria, who was overjoyed to think of Roger escaping the doom that had threatened him, and very proud to think that her father had spoken up so well before the justice. It would be something to remember and talk of for many a long day.

But when Bess, coming home in the evening, heard the good news about Roger, she burst out into a passion of sobs and tears. It was not that Roger was saved, but that David was lost. "Oh, mother, mother!" she cried again and again, "if they'd only done the same by our Davy! And mother always said he'd ha' made a good man, like father!"

Chapter 13. GLAD TIDINGS

It was two or three days after this, when Euclid and Bess had come in from their cress−selling in the evening, that a loud, strange knock at the door of their garret struck alarm into the hearts of all the three. Blackett had not hitherto molested any of them, but they lived in daily terror of him, and some of their neighbours had warned them to look out for danger. Victoria and Bess uttered a low scream, and Euclid shuffled across the floor to fasten the staple; but already a hand had pushed it a little wider open from the outside, and he could see in the dim light that it was a stranger who was standing there, and a stranger not in the dress of a policeman.

"May I come in?" asked a pleasant voice.

"Air you a friend, or air you a enemy?" inquired Euclid.

"A friend surely!" answered the stranger. "My name is Dudley, John Dudley, and I bring you news of Roger Blackett. I saw you and your daughter in the Court the other day."

"Come in, come in!" exclaimed Euclid, throwing the door wide open; "you're kindly welcome."

The daylight still lingered in the garret, and they could see plainly the pleasant yet grave face of the gentleman who entered, and whose simple and easy manner made them feel confidence in him at once. Victoria set the only chair there was for him, and he took it as if he had been a familiar guest, whilst Euclid seated himself on the soap−box and the two girls on the side of the bed. Mr. Dudley looked at them both inquiringly.

"You were frightened when I knocked at the door?" he said.

"Ay, ay!" answered Euclid. "We're all scared a'most to death at Blackett. He's like a ragin' lion, and we canna go in nor out without passin' by his door, sir."

"I'm afraid he'll be worse," said Mr. Dudley, "for he is to pay half−a−crown a week for the keep of his son Roger"

In Prison and Out

"Then we shall ha' to flit somewheres," said Euclid mournfully, "and we've lived here nigh upon ten years, me and Victoria. It's hard upon peaceful folks like us; and Victoria can't take away her pretty picters. Look here, sir, we've been ten year's a–gettin' 'em together, and if we are forced to flit, we must have 'em all behind us."

Above the fireplace, against the wall of the projecting chimney, there was a collection of poor, coarse wood–cuts out of cheap illustrated papers, pasted upon the white-washed plaster close against one another, as they had come into Victoria's possession. Euclid pointed them out with pride, mingled with sorrow as he thought of how these treasures must be left behind, if they were compelled to quit the garret for other lodgings. He sat down with a heavy sigh after calling Mr. Dudley's attention to Victoria's favourite pictures.

"Are you fond of reading as well as of pictures?" asked Mr. Dudley.

"None on us can read," answered Euclid. "Victoria was always too weakly to go to school wi' a lot o' rough lads and lasses; she's so nesh and simple. And little Bess there is no scholar; she gets her livin' like me, sellin' creases. Bess is a old neighbour's child, sir, not mine, and Blackett's hated me ever since I took her to live with me and Victoria. He said he'd make the place too hot for me then; but now—"

He shook his grey head dejectedly, and glanced up at his collection of pictures with a fond and regretful gaze.

"I thought the other day in the Court, when you pleaded for poor Roger, that you must be a religious man," said Mr. Dudley.

"Oh dear, no!" answered Euclid in a surprised tone. "I don't rightly know religion; it's above me, for I'm no scholar. I should like it, may be, if I knew it; and my wife she was a good woman, she was."

"Do you know nothing of our Lord Jesus Christ?" asked Mr. Dudley.

"I've heard the name," he said reflectively. "Oh yes! of course, I've heard the name; but I've had no time to inquire into such things, and they puzzle my head when I hear talk of them. Jesus Christ! Ay, I do know the name well, sir. My wife knew all about Him, I dare say. She died when Victoria were born—poor dear! She could say texts and hymns—lots as I forgot; but some on 'em I remembered long enough to teach 'em to Victoria. Victoria, my dear, do you know anythink o' Lord Jesus Christ?"

"Not much, father," she answered tremulously, as she leaned forward with her pale eager face, gazing at the stranger, who was beginning to talk about what she had often longed to hear.

"You've heard of the Queen?" said Mr. Dudley.

"Ay!" answered Euclid, "there's a many streets and taverns called after her."

"If you heard," continued the stranger in a very quiet, yet clear, impressive voice, "that Queen Victoria was so filled with trouble and sorrow for folks like you, that she had sent her own son, and that he had quite willingly left the splendid and beautiful palace where they live, to come and live in this street here among you, and work for his own bread like all of you are doing, spending all his spare time in teaching the children, and nursing the sick people, and helping the neighbours in every way he could, never growing tired of them, but trying to make them as good as himself—what would you think of him?"

"I'd lay my hands under his feet!" cried Bess in an eager tone.

"There'd be no goodness like that in this world!" said Euclid.

"And if he went on," continued Mr. Dudley, "week after week, month after month, and year after year, never going home to his mother's palace, only sending messages to her from time to time—because he was bent upon making you all as good and as happy as himself, and fitting you to go and live with him as his friends in his own palace—and if some of you loved him, but most of you hated him, and those who hated him raised a mob against him, and killed him, and he had only time to send a last message to Queen Victoria, and the message was, 'Mother, forgive them; they do not know what they are doing.' What should you say to that?"

"There never was such goodness!" exclaimed Euclid, whilst Victoria's dark eyes were fastened on the stranger.

In Prison and Out

"Suppose he was even now in the street, and you heard his voice calling, 'Come to Me, all you that labour and are heavy laden, and I will give you rest,' would you go to him?" asked Mr Dudley.

"I'd follow him to the end of the world!" answered old Euclid, striking his hands together and half rising from his seat, as if to start instantly on his pilgrimage.

"That's one o' mother's texts," said Victoria in a timid voice.

"Yes," continued Mr. Dudley, "they are the words of Jesus Christ, the Son of God. Did you never hear this: 'There is joy in the presence of the angels of God over one sinner that repents?' Do you think that is true?"

"Ay, it must be true," answered Euclid, "for my wife's gone to heaven, and she'll have joy, I know, over Roger, if he turns out good."

"Those are the words of Jesus Christ, the Son of God," said Mr. Dudley. "And now, if you could look down into the street and see such a man that we spoke of, the Queen's son, looking round him sorrowfully on the drunken men and miserable women and wretched children here, and you could hear him say, 'I am come to seek and to save those who are lost,' should you believe him?"

"I should! I should!" said Euclid, with tears in his dim old eyes.

"Jesus Christ said that," continued Mr. Dudley. "And if you could hear Him say to you and Victoria and Bess, 'Let not your hearts be troubled: ye believe in God, believe also in Me. In My Father's house there is plenty of room; I am going to prepare a place for you all. And if I go, I will come again, and take you there Myself, that where I am you may be also.' Tell me, what would you say to that? What would you think of Him?"

"God bless Him!" cried old Euclid, sobbing, whilst Victoria's eyes shone with a bright light, and Bess listened with parted lips.

"The very night before His enemies killed Him, Jesus Christ said that, and left it as a message to every one who should believe in Him," said Mr. Dudley. "What a pity you have not known Him all your lives! 'God so loved the world that He gave His only begotten Son, that whosoever believeth in Him should not perish, but have ever-lasting life.' If you could read, Euclid, there is a small book which tells us all we know of Jesus Christ, the Son of God; and all He said and did is as true for us now as it was then, before His enemies rose against Him, and crucified Him."

"I'm afeard I'm too old to learn now," said Euclid regretfully; "but Victoria there has plenty o' time, if anybody 'ud teach her, and if she's not a-goin' to die soon it 'ud be company for her to have that little book. And Bess must learn somehow. I never knew as Jesus Christ said anything like that, 'Come to Me, poor labourin folks, when your Load's heavy, and I'll give you rest!' and 'There's joy in heaven over sinners when they repent;' and 'I'm come to find and save lost folks Ay, and all the other words you've told us. They don't know what they're doin'.' Ah! that's true. It's true of me, and true of Blackett, and Rodger, and all on us! No, no, we don't know what we're doing."

"I'll find someone to teach Victoria and Bess," said the stranger, "and Roger will be well taught. He is going down the river to the ship *Cleopatra,* where he will be trained as a seaman, and taught how to read and write. I thought you would be glad to know that."

"Oh, if Davy could only ha' gone where Roger's goin'!" said Bess sorrowfully.

Mr Dudley listened attentively to the story of David Fell's crimes against his country and her laws, and the measure of stripes meted out for them and learning the name of the gaol where he was now imprisoned, he went away, promising to see them again soon.

Chapter 14. MRS. LINNETT'S LODGINGS

John Dudley went away with a heavier heart than when he came to bring good news of Roger. If one boy was saved, the other seemed irretrievably lost. He knew too well one inevitable result of sending boys to prison—the forfeiture of their only wealth, the wealth of a good name. If David came out of gaol neither degraded nor corrupted by contact with confirmed criminals, a thing he hardly dared to hope, he would still bear about with him, at the very beginning of his life, the stigma of being a gaol-bird!

Dudley's blood boiled, and his heart ached with mingled indignation and sorrow, as he paced slowly along the narrow and dirty street which had been at once David Fell's school and playground. Scarcely a decent man or woman met his eye, and his ear heard oaths and speeches such as had been the common language surrounding David from his earliest childhood. Yet what had the boy been guilty of? Untaught, untrained, with no instruction but the vile and coarse lessons of a London slum, he had kept true to the only faith he had: his faith in an honest and industrious father. He had striven to his utmost to be honest and industrious, and he had not failed. His crimes had been—begging for his mother when she was dying of hunger; and rescuing—hotly, perhaps, but bravely—a slur upon his mother's good name, when that was maligned by the man who had robbed her.

Misery and degradation and crime lay all about Dudley as he turned homewards, and for the moment it seemed a hopeless task to endeavour to raise this dead mass of city's lowest population from its ignorance and savagery. And what if the law did not aid him! If the best of these young barbarians, yielding to his natural instincts, broke the laws he did not know, and was arrested by a Christian people, not to be wisely and gently dealt with, but to be set for evermore against society, every man's hand against him and his hand against every man, what chance was there for him and his fellow-labourers to work any deliverance?

John Dudley paced along the streets, deep in thought, yet taking unconscious notice of the groups of loafing, ill-fed, ill-clad lads who thronged the causeways. His mind was pondering over a book he had been reading lately; a very popular book, which has been a favourite with all the upper and middle classes of Great Britian. It was "Tom Brown's School Days." The school was Rugby; the head master, Dr. Arnold, a man called to his post by God Himself, and set there as a pattern and example to all schoolmasters. Every boy in the school was the son of a well-to-do, if not a wealthy, father. But oh, the scrapes those boys got into, and got out of! The crimes against English law they committed! Had the same measure been meted to them that every day was meted to these desolate, degraded, uncared-for street lads, how many a brave and worthy English gentleman—ay! and magistrate—of the present day must now have been a greyhaired convict in penal servitude. He had known boys and girls under fifteen years of age sent to gaol for breaking down a rotten fence; for throwing a stone and unintentionally breaking a window; for snatching an apple off a stall, or a penny loaf out of a baker's shop; or for stealing a few turnips from a field, and a handful of corn from a sheaf. But what were these trespasses compared with many committed day after day, by schoolboys in every school in the kingdom? No doubt the schoolboys were punished, but they were not cast, in the name of law and justice, into a gulf from which there was no clear escape in this

In Prison and Out

life.

By-and-by his thoughts turned to old Euclid. It was quite plain that he must move away from his garret, now Blackett's hatred was so greatly provoked. But where must he go? Could nothing better be found than that miserable attic, with its thin roof of slates and lath-and-plaster ceiling, as the sole shelter against the frosts and snows of winter and the hot sun of summer? No wonder that girl looked like a ghost, with her small, wan face, and emaciated frame! Could nothing be done for them?

At last his face brightened, and he turned hastily southwards, towards the river. He went on nearly to the docks, and then entered a short and quiet street. A fresh breeze blew up from the water, chilly enough this February night, but giving promise of a pleasant air on a summer's day. He paused at a little shop with miscellaneous wares displayed in a bay-window with small panes, and with a door divided across the middle, the upper part of which was open. As he pushed open the lower part, a sharp little bell tinkled loudly, and in an instant an elderly woman appeared in the doorway of an inner room.

"I'm coming in, Mrs. Linnett," he said.

The small kitchen beyond the shop was scantily furnished with an arm-chair cushioned with homemade patchwork, two Windsor chairs, a table, and a kitchen-piece, combining a chest of drawers with a cupboard. But the walls were decorated with many cheap foreign curiosities, and over the fireplace hung a highly coloured engraving of a three-master, all sails full set, and four little black figures, representing the crew, standing at equal distances along the bulwarks. A burning mountain in the distance, in a terrific state of eruption, and the intense blue of the sea and sky, suggested the Bay of Naples. Underneath were the words, "Barque *Jemima*. Master, Thomas Linnett."

There was no light in the little kitchen except that of the fire, but there was enough to show the placid and pleasant face of Mrs. Linnett, though it was partially concealed by a green shade over her eyes. John Dudley smiled as he looked at her.

"I think I've found you a little maid," he said, "and a lodger, if I pay a small portion of his rent. He's an honest old fellow, or I'm much mistaken, and he gets his living by selling water-cresses."

In Prison and Out

"It's a poor trade," remarked Mrs. Linnett tranquilly.

"He's as poor as a man can be, and keep off the parish," continued Mr. Dudley; "and he has a daughter, very sickly, who will grow well and happy with a little mothering such as you will give to her. And there's a strong, bright girl, whom they have adopted, and who is the little maid I spoke of."

"Three of 'em!" said Mrs. Linnett.

"You like to have plenty of folks about you," he answered persuasively; "and by-and-by the elder girl will help you to keep shop, and Bess will clean and scrub, and you will be at leisure to be my Bible-woman. You shall teach sick and miserable people what you know about God and our Lord. Jesus Christ."

"And them three—do they know?" inquired Mrs. Linnett.

"They know nothing," he said. "None of them can read, and the old man has only one idea in his head: how he can keep off the parish and bury his children and himself in coffins of their own. Try them, Mrs. Linnett. Old Euclid goes to the market every morning, and Bess might still go with him and bring back a basketful of fruit or vegetables for the shop fresh every day. Only promise me to try them."

"You were pretty sure o' that, afore you came in, Mr. Dudley," she answered, with a quiet laugh. "I couldn't say no to you, as befriended me when Thomas Linnett died, away at sea. Where would my twenty pounds a year ha' been, but for you? There's the front room up-stairs, and a closet as 'ill do for the old man to sleep in, and Bess 'ill sleep with me. I've kep' them for old shipmates o' Thomas Linnett's: but they'll find lodgings close by, and my heart goes after those two young lasses as have everything to learn. They'll fill up my spare time when trade's slack."

"How often is trade slack?" asked Mr. Dudley.

"Not as often as you'd think, sir," she said cheerfully. "Bein' so handy to the docks, there's always some old mate or other droppin' in, as knew Thomas Linnett. They step in here, or if it's fine they sit on the counter, and we talk of old times on the *Jemima;* and most of 'em 'ud spend more money in the shop than I let 'em. Some of 'em leave their money with me for safety, and I've six or seven sea-chests in my room to be took care of. So there's not so much slack time for me as you'd suppose."

Old Euclid visited the new lodgings proposed to him the next day, for there was no time to be lost. Some caution was necessary in making the move, so as to leave no clue by which Blackett could trace them. To make sure of perfect security, the old bedsteads once belonging to Mrs. Fell were privately disposed of, as well as the broken chair and empty boxes. The rest of their possessions were packed up, and stealthily conveyed downstairs at four o'clock in the morning, Euclid's usual hour for being about, and a hand-truck sent by John Dudley quietly carried them off. Later in the morning, Victoria, pale and trembling, descended the familiar staircase for the last time, and, clinging to Bess, passed Blackett's open door. He scowled at them as they went by, and muttered an oath, but he did not rise up to follow them. When they had safely gained the corner of the street, a cab took them up and set them down at Mrs. Linnett's door.

One of the many old shipmates who had sailed in the *Jemima* with Thomas Linnett had papered the front room with a cheerful paper of red roses, and had festooned the window with strings of some foreign beans of a bright scarlet. The old egg-shaped grate, with high hobs, had been polished till it glittered in the firelight. Victoria's bed stood in the corner, ready made, and Euclid's was also ready in a little closet opening at the top of the narrow stairs. Over the chimney-piece hung an oval looking-glass, cracked across the middle, which had once belonged to some ship's cabin, and had found its way into Mrs. Linnett's possession; and on each side of it was a picture in a black frame. Victoria stood on the threshold of this sumptuous dwelling-place, gazing at it with wondering eyes, till she suddenly broke down into tears.

"Oh, it's too grand!" she sobbed. "We can never pay the rent here!"

"To be sure you can," said Mrs. Linnett, soothing her tenderly; "and by-and-by you'll more than pay the rent, my dear, when you are strong enough to help me in the shop; and that won't be long, my poor precious! There's the fresh breeze blowing off the river that 'ill make you strong, and there's me to look after you, poor dear, that never knew what it is to have a mother! And father 'll be as happy as a king to see you picking up your roses. And there's Bess—why, she'll be as good as a fortune to me, I know; she'll save my old legs and arms so! And it's a mile nigher to the market, and Bess shall go and buy me apples and oranges and greengrocery for the shop, and we'll sell all the cresses as Mr.

Euclid brings home of an evening. And you'll see if he doesn't more than pay the rent!"

Chapter 15. AN HOUR TOO SOON

It was a constant marvel to Euclid how Victoria grew stronger and brighter. Presently her pallid cheeks gained a faint tinge of red, and looked fuller and rounder; her eyes were happier and her step less languid. She had no long solitary hours now; even when she was alone in her room she could call Mrs. Linnett or Bess to her at any moment. Unknown to Euclid, Mr. Dudley provided more nourishing food for her than she had ever had in her life, and she was thriving upon it, as well as upon Mrs. Linnett's motherly care. It was like a new life to Victoria.

She learned to read and write with astonishing rapidity, leaving Bess far behind, and filling Euclid's old heart with fatherly pride in her. He could not keep himself from boasting of his daughter's learning to the saleswoman from whom he bought his cresses. His purchases in the market were of more importance now, as he had to keep the shop supplied with fresh fruit and vegetables, and as Mrs. Linnett reckoned his services as worth a shilling a week to her, he felt well paid for his trouble. "The winter's woe was past" in very truth. He had lost his hoarded savings, and would never get them back; but what were they to Victoria's returning health, and the sight of her dear face as it greeted him evening after evening, looking out for him to come home, over the lower half of Mrs. Linnett's shop-door?

The only sorrow that sat by their fireside was the thought of David in prison. Bess was always talking of him, and of the day when he would be discharged. They counted the days till that would come. Old Euclid knew it as well as Bess, and Mr. Dudley pondered over the matter as much as they did. What was to be done with David when he came out of prison? How could the grievous wrong that had been done to him be set right? Could it ever be set right in this world?

"Davy 'ill be out next week," said Bess one evening when they were all gathered round Mrs. Linnett's fire. Bess was sorely troubled. She could never forsake David—that was impossible! But would Euclid and Victoria and Mrs. Linnett be willing to let her go away with him, in his disgrace, and lose sight of her for evermore? She knew too well into what a gulf of misery and degradation she must fall with David, and a strange horror crept over her as she thought of it; but none the less was she ready to go away with him from this pleasant and sure shelter, rather than be guilty of deserting him in his dire distress. No, never could she forsake Davy!

"There's a verse you read last night, Mrs. Linnett," said Old Euclid, "as has been runnin' in my head all day. I've not got the words quite true, I know, ma'am, but it's somethink like this:

'God doesn't want one o' these little young ones to be lost.' Somethink o' that sort it is."

"Ay, I know," answered Mrs. Linnett. "'It is not the will of your Father in heaven that one of these little ones should perish.' Jesus Christ said it; it's His words."

"It's like Him," said Euclid, with a smile on his grey face; "it seems as if He was always a–sayin' somethink beautiful. And just afore that there was somethink about a sheep going astray, and gettin' lost on the mountains, and how He'd rejoice over it when it was found again; and then He says it's the same with the little ones; they shan't perish either. Poor Davy! he's gone astray, and he's no more than a young lamb as doesn't know the right way. What are we to do to set him right again, so as he shouldn't perish? If it's God's will, it must be done, I reckon."

"Where should Davy go but here?" asked Mrs. Linnett, in a hearty, cheery voice, which made the downcast heart of poor Bess leap for joy. "If you and he 'ud sleep together in my bed, Bess shall have the closet, and I'll sleep with Victoria. We shall shake down somehow. And Captain Upjohn, my old shipmate, says he'll take him away to Sweden, and they'll be away six weeks or more, and his hair 'ill be grown, and he'll look all right when he gets back. Maybe he'll take to a seafaring life, and then he'll get on well, I know."

"Oh, if mother only knew!" cried Bess.

The day before David's release from gaol was a great day in Mrs. Linnett's little house. Bess scrubbed every floor, and rubbed every article of furniture, as if they could not be bright enough to give David a welcome. All the while she was thinking of the many things she would have to tell him; of Roger's theft, and Blackett's hatred, and of Mr. Dudley and Mrs. Linnett, and this new happy home in which she found herself. Mrs.

In Prison and Out

Linnett, who dearly loved a little festival, was making wonderful preparations for a dinner far beyond a common meal to-morrow; and Victoria was helping her to wash currants and stone raisins for a pudding. None of them spoke much of the coming event, though their hearts were full of it; for lying beneath the gladness there ran a strong under-current of grief for the past, and of vague dread of the future.

"I wish Jesus Christ was only here now!" cried Bess, flinging her arms round Mrs. Linnett's neck, and sobbing on her shoulder. "I'd go and tell Him every word about Davy, and ask Him if He thought him bad enough to be sent to gaol. If He was livin' anywhere in London, I'd crawl to Him on my hands and knees if I couldn't walk, and tell Him all about it."

"He knows all about it, Bess," answered Mrs. Linnett, "and He'll make it up to him in some way. Only I wonder, I do wonder, as Christian folks can let it be! If the Queen 'ud only think about it, or the grand Lords and the Commons, as the newspapers speak about, they'd never let it be, I know. They'd find some other way to punish children. But we'll try and make Davy forget it when he comes home."

Mr. Dudley had found out the usual hour for the discharge of prisoners, and it was settled that Euclid and Bess should be waiting for him when the outer door of the gaol was opened. Bess was awake long before it was time to get up that morning. It was an April day, six full calendar months since David had left home in the autumn to go begging for his mother. Euclid had time to make his early round, and sell his cresses for the working-men's breakfasts; and he had resolved to make the rest of the day a holiday. Bess met him as he had just finished his sales, and then they turned their steps in the direction of the City prison. They were both happier and gayer than they had been since David went away, but Bess was especially glad. For, after all, in spite of the sorrow which cast so deep a shadow over her life, still David was coming back to her, and he was her own. He belonged to her, and she belonged to him. And Davy had always been so good to her.

They reached the prison a few minutes before the appointed hour, and paced up and down under its gloomy walls, blackened with dust and smoke, and towering high above the bent old man and half-grown girl who trod half timidly under their shadow. The heavy gates were shut close, and no sound was to be heard beyond them. The porter's closely barred window and thick door seemed to forbid them to knock there and make any

In Prison and Out

inquiry. But they had none to make.

They continued to pace to and fro patiently, with the meek and quiet patience of most of the honest and decent poor, not expecting any notice to be taken of them, nor wishing to give any trouble. To and fro, to and fro, until the nearest church clock and the gaol clock within the walls struck an hour behind the time, and still the prisoners were not set free. Again the weary footsteps trod beneath the gloomy shadows, and both Euclid and Bess fell into an almost unbroken and anxious silence. How was it that David was still kept in prison?

At length the door of the porter's lodge was opened, and a warder came out, having it instantly and jealously closed after him. Old Euclid summoned courage enough to address him.

"Sir," he said respectfully, "is there anything gone wrong inside the gaol?"

"Why do you want to know?" inquired the warder, with a sharp glance at them both; "what are you hanging about here for?"

"We are waitin' for this lassie's brother—David Fell," he answered, whilst Bess gazed up eagerly yet timidly into the warder's face; "his time's up to–day, and we've been looking out for him to take him home with us."

"Why, the prisoners have been gone this two hours," replied the warder. "We let them out an hour earlier than usual, for we've got some great visitors coming to see the gaol, and we wanted to get on with business. They didn't make any objections, not one of 'em, I can tell you. You make haste home, and you'll find him there."

But Euclid and Bess knew that they could not find David at Mrs. Linnett's, and they retraced their homeward path sadly and heavily. If he had thought of going to any home, it must be to that old, unhappy place, where his mother had died the day after his second conviction, and thither neither Euclid nor Bess dared follow for fear of Blackett. It was six weeks since they had secretly quitted it, and not a soul among their old neighbours knew where they had found a new roof to shelter them. They had trusted no one with that precious secret.

Yet Bess could not bear the thought of losing David. They must not lose him. Alas! they guessed too well where he must be. But how could they get to him, and let him know what friends and what a home were waiting to welcome him?

The feast was ready by the time they reached home, but none of them had a heart for it. Mrs. Linnett, however, took a cheerful view of the misfortune, and assured them Mr. Dudley would know how to find David without bringing any danger to Euclid. Mr. Dudley looked in during the evening, and upon hearing the news started off at once in search of David. He was almost as anxious to find the lad and take him home as Bess herself could have been.

David had been at the old house—that was quickly and easily learned. He had knocked at two doors, and been driven away from them, both as a thief and a gaol-bird, but nobody could tell where he had gone to. At last Mr. Dudley made an inquiry at Blackett's own door; but all he could learn was that Blackett himself had left his old lodgings for good that very day, and had taken cares not to leave his address.

Chapter 16. TWICE IN GAOL

For the second time, or as the prison report registered it, for the third time, David Fell had been committed to gaol for three months. David knew the prison report was wrong. More than this, he did not feel that his first offence had deserved so severe a penalty. Now, when he had been defending his mother's good name, and seeking the restoration of her property, his whole boyish nature rose rebelliously under a sense of cruel injustice.

He would do it again he cried within himself; yes, if all the magistrates and policemen in the whole world were looking on. Why should his mother be cheated out of the only treasure that she possessed? and how could he stand by and hear her called what Mr. Quirk had called her? His mother was as good as any woman in London, and he was ready to fight anybody who gave her an ill name.

He was but a boy still. In many homes he would have been reckoned among the children, and his faults of temper would have been passed over, or leniently dealt with. He was in gaol for a brave, rash action, which most men would have applauded in their own sons. Each time the trial that consigned him to an imprisonment of three months had not

In Prison and Out

occupied more than five minutes. Police–courts are busy places, with a constant pressure of affairs to be dispatched, and a police–magistrate has not time to investigate the statements of boys, who, nine times out of ten, are telling a lie in order to escape punishment. David had been caught red–handed in his transgression of the law; and the law, framed as it had been against wrong–doers, swept him in its resistless current into gaol.

The prison was not the one from which he had just been released, but there was a mournful sameness to it. He did not feel like a stranger there. He had had one night free—a night and a day with his dying mother; and now three more months stretched before him. But this time he was sullen and moody, brooding over his injuries. There was no longer the hope to sustain him of learning a trade by which he could maintain his mother and Bess. He felt sure his mother would be dead before his second term was over, and it would be best for little Bess to have nothing to do with a brother who had been twice in gaol.

David became insolent and refractory. What did it matter if they put him into the black hole, where no single ray of light could enter? The darkness could not affright him; or, if it did, he would harden himself against it, as he hardened himself against every punishment or expostulation. He was honest and truthful—yet he was branded a thief and a liar. He was intensely ignorant—yet he was punished for actions which would have been applauded in a gentleman's son. He could not put his wretchedness into words; you might as well ask of him to paint on canvas a picture of his prison–cell. His tongue was dumb, but his memory and the passion of his heart were never silent. They were for ever muttering to him in undertones of revenge, and hatred, and defiance.

David completed his fourteenth year in gaol. The heavy–browed sullen–faced boy, who was discharged from his second imprisonment in April, could hardly have been recognised as the lad who had gone out, ashamed though resolute, to beg for help the preceding October. He slouched along the sunny streets, under the blue sky, bright with glistening spring clouds, but he paid no heed to sunshine or cloud. In old times there had been the changes of the seasons even for him and little Bess, in their squalid street, but they had no more power over his sullen moods. He sauntered on, not homewards—he knew too well there could be no home for him—but towards the old familiar place, the only spot he knew well on earth, where at least he would find faces not altogether strange to him, if they were not the faces of friends, and where alone he could learn any tidings of

In Prison and Out

Bess. But he did not hurry. There was no mother now to be hungry for a sight of him.

Still, when he reached the house he went straight to the old door and knocked. A stranger opened it, and looked suspiciously at him. There was no Mrs. Fell there; she had never heard of such a person. She had only come into the house three weeks ago, and she was too busy getting her own living to go gossiping among the neighbours. She slammed the door to in his face, and he heard her draw the bolt on the inside. He had not caught even a glimpse of the poor, dark room which had once been his home.

"I'll go up-stairs and ask Victoria," said David to himself.

He mounted the stairs slowly and quietly, not with the buoyant step of an active and restless lad, but with the hesitating, listless tread of a culprit. He was ashamed of facing either Euclid or Victoria, and he was almost afraid that their door would be shut in his face. But when he reached the foot of the last staircase, leading only to their garret, he saw the door open, and he mounted more quickly.

Yes, the door was open, propped open with a brick, to prevent it from banging to and fro on its hinges. But the garret was quite empty. There was no trace left of its former tenants, except the pictures which Victoria had pasted over the fireplace. All was gone; the broken chair, the corner cupboard, the poor flock-bed from the floor, the black kettle, and little brown tea-pot; there was nothing left. David sat down in the corner where Victoria's bed had been, and hid his face in his hands. If there had been a faint hope left in his heart of finding friends and a refuge here, the glimmer of it died away into utter darkness. He was absolutely alone in the world which had been so cruel to him.

It is possible that he fell asleep for very sorrow; but after a long while, as the dusk of evening was creeping on, he roused himself and slowly descended the stairs. On the second floor he tapped with a trembling hand on a closed door, and quietly lifted the latch. He knew the workman, who lived there with his wife and children. They were sitting at supper; and the man, calling out "Who's there?" looked up, as David put his pale face round the door.

"I'm looking for my mother!" he said in a faltering voice.

In Prison and Out

"Your mother!" repeated the man, rising angrily, "I know what you want, you gaol-bird. Get out o' this at once, you skulking thief!"

But David did not wait for him to reach the door. He closed it hastily, and ran down-stairs to escape if he was pursued. As he was passing into the street he heard his name called through Blackett's open door. He stopped instantaneously, catching at a straw of hope. Perhaps Roger could tell him what had become of Bess.

"Come in, David Fell," called the voice of Blackett himself, "come in; now you're tarred with the same stick as my lads, you needn't stand off from me no more. You and me 'ill be as thick as thieves now. Come in, my lad," he added, in as kindly a tone as he could assume, "I'm right sorry for thee, and I've news for thee."

For a moment David hesitated, remembering his mother's dread of her neighbour; but Blackett came to the door, and dragged him in, in no way roughly.

"You've come to look after your poor mother?" he said gravely.

David nodded.

"She's dead—died the very night after you was booked for another three months," said Blackett.

David did not speak. No change passed over his hard and sullen face. He had known it all the while, in the dreary solitude of his prison cell; he would never see his mother's face again; never! Yet as he stood there, opposite to Blackett, he felt as if he could see her, lying in the room beyond, on the sacking of her comfortless bed, with her white face and hungry eyes turned towards the door, watching for him to come in.

"And Bess is gone away—nobody knows where," continued Blackett, eyeing the boy with a keen, sinister gaze, "on the streets somewhere. There's not much chance for Bess, neither."

David flinched and shivered. Should he ever see little Bess again? Never again as he had been used to see her. He could recollect all his life through having her given into his care and keeping, a younger, smaller, feebler creature dependent upon him. He had played

In Prison and Out

with her and fought for her; they had eaten and been hungry together, and had had every event of their lives in common, until he was sent to gaol. Was little Bess likely to be sent to gaol too? Girls as young as Bess were sent to prison, and the chances were all against her keeping out of it.

"Queen Victoria and my Lord Euclid are gone," went on Blackett with a sneer; "they made a moonlight flit of it, and they hadn't the manners to leave their address behind 'em. They carried all their fortune with them."

Still David did not speak, but stood looking into Blackett's face with a forlorn and listless strangeness, which touched even him with its utter loss of hope.

"Come, come, my lad, never say die!" he exclaimed. "Take a drop out o' my glass here, and pluck up your spirits. Take a good pull at it, David. You haven't asked after Roger? He's in better luck than you. He cribbed a parcel of money from under Victoria's pillow, and my Lord Euclid had him took up for it. I was always in hopes of gettin' him off my hands, the poor hang-dog! but he had grand luck. Old Euclid sets to and pleads for him to the justice, and they found out as it was a sin and a shame to send a lad like him to gaol; a lad o' fourteen! And they've sent him to school! To school, David, where he's quite the gentleman!"

But here David broke into a loud and very bitter cry. Why had they not done the same with him? Oh! why had they committed him to gaol, and sent Roger to school? He hid his face in his hands, and hot tears of anger and despair rolled down his cheeks.

"They've made an order on me for half-a-crown a week," continued Blackett, after a pause. "I've paid it six weeks, and now I'm giving 'em the slip. I'm agoing to cross the river into Surrey to-night, and if you'll come along with me, I'll say you are my son, and I'll pay your lodgin' to-night; an old neighbour's son sha'n't sleep in the streets. Come, David! You haven't got another friend in this place, and I don't ask you to be a thief. You shall get your living quite honest if you can. You're not a lazy hound like Roger, or I'd have nought to say to you. But you'll always be worth your bread and cheese, if you can get work. Come, and we'll get supper at the tavern afore we start."

"I'll come," said David. At the word supper he felt how hungry he was; and he remembered that he was penniless. Blackett had already disposed of his few possessions to the tenant who had taken his room; so there was nothing now to be done but to pick up his bundle of clothes, and his glazier's tools, and, as it was already night, to take his departure across the river, where he was as yet unknown by sight to the police. David Fell followed him as his only friend.

Chapter 17. MEETING AND PARTING

Blackett was as good as his word. He did not in any way interfere with David's efforts to obtain work by which he could live honestly. He counted surely upon what the result would be; and when he saw David start off morning after morning on his fruitless search, he would thrust his tongue into his cheek, and chuckle scornfully, causing the lad's heavy heart to sink yet lower. But no one else was kind to him; and though he had a lurking dread and distrust of Blackett, there was no one else to give him a morsel of food. Blackett gave him both food and shelter, and of an evening he took him with him to the haunts of men like himself, and amongst them David perfected the lessons he had begun to learn in gaol.

The brave spirit of the boy was broken; his powers of endurance were gone. He could no longer bear the gnawings of hunger and the cravings of thirst, as he had done as long as he could hold up his head before any one of his fellow-men. He felt compelled to slink away from the eye of a policeman, fancying that all the force knew him. And he had indeed the indelible brand of the prison-house upon him. He had a sullen, hang-dog expression, a skulking, cowardly gait, an alarmed eye, and restless glance, looking out for objects of dread. When he was hungry—and how often that was!—he no longer hesitated to snatch a slice of fish or a bunch of carrots from a street-stall, if he had a good chance of escape. To march whistling along the streets, with his head well up and his step free, was a thing altogether of the past now.

He made no effort to find Bess. If there had been any faint, forlorn hope in his heart, when he left gaol, of still doing something better than drifting back into it, it had died away entirely before he had been a fortnight with Blackett. The courage he had once had was transformed into a reckless defiance of the laws and the society that had dealt so cruelly with him. What did he owe to society? Why should he keep its laws? He soon learned to say that his consent had not been asked when they were made, and why should he be bound by them? A rich man's son had all his heart could desire, and might break

In Prison and Out

many of the laws of the land, because he could afford to pay a fine for it; whilst he, David Fell, left by society to live in degradation and forced idleness, was hurried off to prison for innocent offences such as his had been. A strong sense of injury and injustice smouldered in his boyish heart.

Summer came and went, and a second winter dragged down the poor again to their yearly depths of suffering and privation. David was in gaol once more, this time for theft, at which he laughed. Prison was a comfortable shelter from the cold and hunger of the dreary mid-winter; and if he had only luck enough to keep out of it in the summer, it was not bad for winter quarters. He learned more lessons in shoemaking, by which he could not get an honest living outside the gaol-walls among honest folk. The time for that was past. He did not try to find work when he was free again. Henceforth the work David's hands would find to do was what God's law as well as man's law, Christ as well as the world, call crime. But whose fault was it?

Nearly a year and a half had passed since Euclid and Victoria and Bess had found a home with Mrs. Linnett, and though Mr. Dudley had done all in his power to discover David, every effort had failed. One July evening Bess was crossing London Bridge. The light from the setting sun shone upon the river, which was rippling in calm, quiet lines, with the peaceful flowing in of the tide. Bess stood still for a few minutes, gazing westward to the golden sky. She was a prettier girl than even her own mother had thought sadly of her becoming. But this evening her face was brighter than usual; her eyes sparkled, and her lips half parted with a smile, as her thoughts dwelt on some pleasant subject, apart from the beauty of the sunset. She took no notice of the loungers on each side of her, who, like herself, were leaning over the parapet of the bridge and gazing down on the river. But as she roused herself from her pleasant girlish reverie and turned away to go on homewards, a hand was laid on her arm, and a voice beside her said in a low tone, "Bess!"

She started in a tremor of hope and gladness. It was David's voice; his, whom she had sought for in vain ever since she had lost him! But as she looked at him, with her parted lips and shining eyes, a change crept over her face. Could this scampish, vile, and ill-looking lad be David? Yet as she gazed at him a change passed over his face also. His hard, sullen mouth softened, and behind the reddened and bleared eyes there dawned something of the old tender light of the love he had borne for her when she was his little Bess.

In Prison and Out

"Davy!" she cried.

"Ay!" he said.

Then there was a silence. What could they say to one another? There seemed a great gulf between them. They stood side by side; the one simple, and innocent, and good—the other foul, and vicious, and guilty. How far apart they felt themselves to be!

"Davy," said Bess at last, though falteringly, "you must come home with me."

"No," he answered sorrowfully, "I'll never spoil your life, little Bess. You're all right, I see; you've not gone wrong, and I'll never come across you. I'm very glad I've seen you once again, but I didn't try. Bess, I'd ha' been very proud of you if things had happened different."

"Where do you live now?" asked Bess, letting her hand fall upon his greasy sleeve for a moment, but as quickly removing it with a girlish disgust.

"I live off and on with Blackett," he answered. "I've got no other friend in the world; and sometimes he's good enough, and sometimes he's 'ragious. Bess." and he lowered his voice again to a whisper, "I were in gaol again last winter!"

"Oh, Davy! Davy!" she moaned.

"Ay!" he went on; "it's the only home I've got, except the workhouse, and gaol's the best. So I must keep away from you, or I'd do you harm. Don't you tell me where you live, or I'd be a–comin' to look at you sometimes, and it 'ud do you harm, little Bess, and do me no good."

"Oh! if Mr. Dudley 'ud only come by!" Bess cried.

"Who's Mr. Dudley?" asked David.

"He'd find you somewhere to go to, and honest work to do," she answered. "I know he would! and you'd grow up into a good man yet, like father!"

In Prison and Out

"A good man, like father!" he repeated; "no, I couldn't now, I've grown to like it. I like drink, and games, and things as they call wickedness. I can't never be anythink but a thief. There's good folks like you and mother and father; but I've been drove among wicked folks like Blackett; and I can never be like you no more. Mother was a good woman, and what did she come to? Why, she died o' clemming, Blackett's alway a–sayin' so; and he's right there. But she couldn't keep me out o' gaol; and I belong to bad folks now."

"Oh, Davy! Davy!" wailed Bess.

"Good–bye, little Bess," he said, very mournfully; "I don't want ever to see you again. If Blackett was to see you now! No, no, Bess; you and me are parted for evermore. If there's a hell, I'm goin' to it; and if there's a heaven, you're goin' to it! So good–bye, Bess."

"Oh! why doesn't Mr. Dudley come by?" cried Bess again, not knowing what to do. For if David was living with Blackett, she must hide from him where Euclid and Victoria had found shelter from their old enemy. How could she take David home or even tell him where it was, if that would bring danger to them?

"Why did they send me to gaol, and send Roger to school?" said David with bitterness; "it isn't fair. He'd stole money, and I'd only been a beggin' for mother. They didn't give me no chance; and Roger 'll get taught everythink. Nobody can help me now. I'm not sixteen yet, and I've been three times in gaol; and nobody ever taught me how to get a livin' till I went to gaol; and what's the use o' learning any trade *in gaol?* Nobody 'ill take you on when they know where you've been. Father was a good man, and he'd not ha' been willin' to work side by side with a gaol–bird. It stands to reason, Bess. So I can never get free from bad folks, never again."

"What must I do?" cried Bess, weeping, and pressing his arm between both her hands. "Oh, Davy! I can't let you go; but I mustn't take you home with me. What am I to do?"

"Well! only kiss me once," he answered, "just once, and let me go. You can't do nothing for me; it's too late! I'm bad, and a thief now, and all I've got afore me is gaol, gaol! I wouldn't like to spoil your life for you, little Bess. Don't say where you live; don't! It 'ud be too hard for me some day, and I might come after you and spoil your life. Don't forget Davy. Kiss me, Bess! kiss me just once, and let me go!

In Prison and Out

She lifted up her pretty, girlish face to him with lowered eyelids and quivering mouth, and he pressed his hot feverish lips upon it. Then he suddenly wrenched his arm from her grasp, and, running very swiftly, was lost to her sight in a few moments amid the crowd always crossing London Bridge.

Chapter 18. A RED-LETTER DAY

Why had not Mr. Dudley crossed London Bridge at the time when he was so sorely needed? He asked himself this question with a sharp sense of disappointment and defeat. It was custom frequently of an evening to go there and see the sunset on the river, but this day he had felt too busy to go. Some trifling task which could have been done at any other hour had hindered him from attaining an end which he had kept steadily before him ever since he had heard David's history.

He had made every effort to trace David, but had utterly failed hitherto; but the story Bess told, with many tears, brought fresh hope to him. Bess had seen and spoken with him, and learned that he was living with Blackett. There would be less difficulty in tracking out Blackett, who had made himself notorious for many years, than in finding David, whose downward career of vice and crime was but lately begun.

The next day was to be a great and memorable day in the lives of both Victoria and Bess. They had been thinking and dreaming of it for weeks. Mr. Dudley was going to take them down the river to the ship *Cleopatra,* where Roger had been in training for a seaman during the last eighteen months. He had been a troublesome lad at first; cunning and idle, yet with a germ of good in him, which had turned towards David's mother, and had fastened upon her honesty as a quality to be loved and imitated. There had been a careful, kindly, and sympathetic care taken of him by the officers on the *Cleopatra,* and both idleness and cunning had been conquered. But to allow him to return to a land life in London would have been probably to doom him, like David Fell, to a course of guilt, which must lead him to the workhouse or the gaol. His life would be given to England in aiding to carry on her commerce with foreign shores.

The sunrise was as splendid as the sunset had been the night before. Euclid, as he started off to market, called to Victoria out of the street that it was the finest morning of all the year; and long before the right time for starting, Bess and Victoria were down on London

In Prison and Out

Bridge Pier waiting for Mr. Dudley's arrival. When he came Bess pointed out to him the exact spot where she had met David last night, and a cloud shadowed her bright face for a few minutes. But it passed away gradually, as the vessel steamed off and carried her out of sight of the Bridge.

A number of people on the steamer were bound for the *Cleopatra,* for it was the yearly fête day. They could see the ship long before they reached it, standing out clearly against the deep blue of the summer sky, with banners and streamers flying from every mast and along every line of rigging. A boat, manned by *Cleopatra* boys, was waiting at the landing-stage to carry the visitors across to the ship; sunburnt, healthy, bright-eyed lads in navy-blue, looking already like real seamen. One of the biggest of them, as he saw Bess staring about her every way except in his direction, gave a gladsome little shout to call her eyes towards him. It was Roger.

From that moment Bess seemed to see nothing but Roger. So tall he had grown, so strong and bright; his face had lost its scared and sulky look, and smiled whenever he caught her gaze as he bent over his oar, and pulled away, with the other lads, to the ship's side. Roger helped her up the ladder, and made her promise not to go anywhere till he had finished his turn of rowing to and fro to the landing-stage, and was ready to guide her over the *Cleopatra* himself. She and Victoria stood looking over the gunwale at the gay little boats flitting about; whilst the ship's banners and streamers fluttered overhead, and a band of music, played by other boys, sounded joyously from the dock, as boat-load after boat-load of friends and visitors boarded the ship. Bess clasped Victoria's hand very tightly, but she could not speak.

Every steamer brought fresh guests, and the trips to the landing-stage were very numerous; but after a while Roger was at liberty to take Bess triumphantly over the *Cleopatra,* priding himself on the knowledge he had of a hundred things of which she knew nothing. Beneath the main-deck the yearly banquet was spread, on long, narrow tables, profusely decorated with flowers and fruit, and displaying more glass and china than Bess had ever dreamed of. But Roger did not linger there. There was the forecastle to be shown, and the cabins and the school-room, and the boys' sleeping-berths, where Roger hung up his hammock, and leaped into it, coiled himself up in it, and leaped out of it, with an agility which amazed Bess. Above deck were the masts, and the rigging, and the shrouds and boats; and Bess must be told the use of them, and see Roger climbing barefoot, as swiftly as a monkey, till he shouted her name at a giddy height above her, and loosing his hands from the mast, held on by his feet only, to her great agony and dread. And the sun that day shone as Bess had never known it shine before; and the soft winds played about her face, bringing a deeper colour to her cheeks; and but for one heavy sorrow in her inmost heart, she would have been perfectly happy.

Bess and Victoria and Roger had a pleasant little lunch of biscuit and cheese, under a hatchway, by themselves, while the banquet was going on below. After that was over, the prizes were to be given, and behold! Roger had won some of these prizes, and had to step forward before all the crowd of guests and shipmates, very proud yet very shamefaced, to receive them! A hearty cheer rang in his ears as he returned to Bess to show her what he had won, and she saw the tears in his eyes for an instant, though he wiped them away quickly, and cheered the next boy with all his might and strength.

Then there came a number of exercises; and the *Cleopatra* seemed all alive with brisk lads, reefing and furling the sails, running races up the rigging to the mast–head, splicing and knotting ropes, drilling and a variety of wonderful performances, in which Roger was distinguishing himself, while Bess looked on, as if she could gaze for ever. Could this indeed be Roger, the dirty, slouching, miserable boy, who used to creep out of his father's sight into her mother's room? Was he the frightened thief who had stolen Euclid's hoard of money, and who had been saved from gaol by Euclid's earnest pleading? Or was she dreaming a splendid dream, which would fade away as soon as she awoke?

Victoria enjoyed this red–letter day to the full as much as Bess, though she sat still more, and looked most at the deep blue of the sky, and the sparkling of the swift river, and the green meadows sloping down to its margin. She had grown stronger; but she would always be a small and delicate woman, not fit for rough work. Mr. Dudley had been very busy from the moment he had set his foot on board; but when the exercises began, he came to sit down beside her for a little while, thinking to himself how serious yet tranquil her pale face was, and what a quiet smile dwelt in her eyes.

"Anything the matter, Victoria?" he asked.

"I am only thinking, sir," she answered. "I got used to thinking, when father was away all day, and I was left alone, before you knew us."

"And what are you thinking of?" he inquired.

In Prison and Out

"Do it cost more to keep Roger here than to keep David in gaol?" she asked, turning her serious face to him.

"Gaols cost more than training–ships," he answered.

"Roger 'ill know how to get his own livin'," she went on, "and he'll marry a wife, and keep her and his children decent; and he'll never cost anybody no more. But David! I'm thinkin' how he told Bess there's no hope for him now. And, oh! he was so much better than Roger to start with. There was no more harm in him than in Bess then! She'd have turned out bad, if you hadn't found us out in time; all through Roger stealing that money!"

Victoria's eyes filled with tears, and she turned her face half–way from Mr. Dudley, looking sorrowfully towards the sunny west, where the purple smoke of London hung in the sky.

"Did you ever read all through the Gospel of St. Luke, sir?" she asked.

"To be sure, Victoria," he replied.

"Then you've read how when Jesus was come near London, He looked at it, and wept over it. Wept means real crying, doesn't it?"

"Yes," he answered.

"Then Jesus cried over London," she went on; "that was real crying, I know. He only saw the city once, and then He wept over it. I'm thinkin' of that."

"Ah! the city!" he repeated, "yes! 'He beheld the city, and wept over it.' Those are the words, Victoria?"

"Yes," she said.

"It's true of London," he continued, "as true as it ever was of any city in the world. And after Jesus had wept over it, He said, 'If thou hadst known, even thou, at least in this thy day, the things which belong to thy peace! but now they are hid from thine eyes!

In Prison and Out

He stood up, and looked, as she was doing, westward, at the cloud of dun-coloured purple hanging over the city, with the golden beams of the sun already tinging it with crimson light. He knew well, but knew also that not a hundredth part was known to him, what untold sorrows and sins lay underneath that cloud; what ignorance, and degradation, and crime were stalking in visible forms along its streets. He thought of the gaols and the workhouses being enlarged from time to time for the upspringing, and yet unborn, generations of criminals and paupers, which would eat away its glory and its strength. And from the very depths of his heart, he cried, "Would to God thou wouldst learn, in this thy day, the things that belong to thy peace!"

They returned home in a steamer chartered for the purpose of conveying all the guests of the *Cleopatra*. As they dropped away from the training-ship, they were followed by the sound of music; the boys clambered up into the shrouds and stood along the gunwale, and on every point where there was a foothold, waving their shining hats and cheering vociferously as their guests departed. Bess never took her eyes from the ship, and from Roger standing amid his mates, as long as she could see them. It had been a wonderful day; a day to remember as long as she lived. But oh, if David had been there as well as Roger!

Their first landing-place was London Bridge. It was already growing dusk, and the lamps were lit; and as she looked up she fancied she saw David's sad despairing face leaning over the parapet above, and gazing down upon her. But when she looked again it was gone.

Chapter 19. VICTORIA'S WEDDING

It was months before Mr. Dudley could learn anything of David, and then he discovered him in gaol again, for theft of a more serious character. He obtained permission to visit him, and had a long interview with him, and left promising to be his friend. When his term was up Mr. Dudley found him lodgings, and did his best to find him work; but there was no remunerative work to be procured for him, and he was now utterly averse to hard labour with poor pay. It was more than three years since his first committal to prison, and he had learned one lesson so well there that he was no longer willing to bear with starvation or excessive toil. He had nothing to lose by being a thief, except his liberty, and his liberty was equally forfeit if he gave himself to unintermittent labour. His sole

In Prison and Out

ambition now was to thieve so skilfully as to defy the vigilance of his enemies—the police.

There was, at least, one point of good left in him. He would not hear where Bess was living, and begged Mr. Dudley not to tell her of his lost condition. "Let me go down to hell alone," he said: "I'm not afeard of it, but I don't want to see little Bess there!" It was in vain that Mr. Dudley reasoned with him, and entreated him to try again. How could he try again? Would anything ever alter the shameful fact that he had been several times in gaol? Or would any effort take away his name from the terrible list of habitual criminals kept by the police? The name his father bore, and his mother loved, David Fell, was inscribed there.

"This is a damned world," he said, one day to Mr. Dudley. He had been speaking of his mother and little Bess, and the tears had started to his eyes. But suddenly, as if some smouldering fire within had been stirred anew, a fierce flame burned in his eyes, and scorched up the healing tears. Mr. Dudley did not know what to answer.

It was well for Bess that Mr. Dudley kept David's secret, and said nothing to her of his failure in trying to redeem him. Roger had entered the merchant-service, and was serving before the mast in a sailing vessel that went long voyages, and came into London Docks but seldom. When he was on shore his home was always at Mrs. Linnett's, where old Euclid took a pride in him as being a lad saved from destruction through his mediation; yet there was always a little dread mingled with his welcome visits, lest Blackett should come across his son, and so discover the refuge they had found from his hatred and revenge.

It had become a standing joke at the market, and amongst Euclid's oldest and familiar customers, that the old water-cress seller must have come into a fortune, so changed was he. He looked as if the old bent in his shoulders was growing straighter, and his bowed-down head more erect. The linen-blouse he had always worn as his outer garment was no longer ragged or dirty; and in the winter a warm, though threadbare, great-coat took its place. He had become a very independent buyer, and most fastidious in his choice of cresses. No fear now that he must put up with any cresses gone yellow at the edges, or spotted on the bright green leaf. He could pay for the best, and the saleswomen knew that he would have the best. He could afford to give more liberal and larger bunches, and his wrinkled face did not fall into abject disappointment if he was asked to give credit for a day or two. He was quite another being from the stooping, shuffling, poverty-stricken, decrepid old man, who had been wont to cry, "Creshe, creshe!" in a hoarse and mournful voice along the streets.

It was the home he and Victoria had found which did it. There was a nourishing warmth in the sense of friendship and fellow-feeling which surrounded him there. Mrs. Linnett's cheery ways, and Mr. Dudley's kindly interest in them, made him feel that they were no longer alone in the battle of life. If he fell on the battle-field, Victoria would not be trampled under foot in its fierce conflict. There was the same hard toil for him; the chilly mornings of winter were no warmer; but the world appeared quite another place to him, for his heart was no longer heavy nor his spirit cast down.

It had been strongly urged upon Roger by Mr. Dudley and by his teachers on board the *Cleopatra* that he must replace the money he had formerly stolen from Euclid. This purpose became a secret between him and Bess and Mrs. Linnett, who delighted in innocent surprises. When the sum was completed, on his return from his second voyage, he and Bess tied it up in an old handkerchief and placed it under Victoria's pillow, where her Testament was often laid now, that she might be reading it in the early light of the morning, as soon as Bess and her father began to stir. Victoria's hand, groping for her litttle book, grasped the old well-remembered parcel of hard money, and she screamed, "Father! father!" till Euclid appeared at the door, looking in with a terrified face.

"It's the money for my coffin come again!" she cried, bursting into tears.

"No, no!" said Bess, between laughing and crying. "It's the money as Roger stole, every penny of it, saved up to be given back to you, with his love! Oh, Roger, tell them! tell them all about it!"

But Roger, who was standing behind Euclid at the door, could not utter a word. It felt to him a happier time even than when he had received his prizes, in the presence of all his mates. Old Euclid's face, bewildered and alarmed at first, changed into a joyous and radiant delight.

"Nigh upon four pounds!" he said. "Well done, Roger! But I don't know how we're to spend it, Victoria, my dear. It's not wanted for your buryin'."

In Prison and Out

"It's for her weddin' wi' Captain Upjohn!" called out Roger, with a chuckle of delight, whilst Euclid laughed hoarsely, and Mrs. Linnett joined him, as Victoria cried—"Father, shut the door!

It was true. Captain Upjohn, the master of a sloop trading to and from Sweden, and an old shipmate of Thomas Linnett, though many years younger, was about to make Victoria his wife. No fear now that she would ever have to rough it, little and tender as she was. Captain Upjohn would see to that; and he would see to old Euclid himself, and provide a home for him when it was no longer possible for him to earn his own bread. There was some talk already of setting him up with a donkey-cart, and so putting him into a larger and more respectable a way of living; for Captain Upjohn was a man who should have married in a higher rank than that of water-cress sellers, and would have done it if he had not met with Victoria at Mrs. Linnett's, and thought so much of her as to forget her father's low estate.

Proud and happy beyond words was old Euclid when his last and only child, Victoria, was married, and he led her to church, her dear hand in his, to give her away to Captain Upjohn, instead of following her to the grave, as he had followed her mother, and all his other children. He knew the burial service well, or rather he knew the ceremony of a funeral, for the words had made little impression on him; but a wedding was new to him. He could dimly remember what he said when he married Victoria's mother; and as Captain Upjohn and Victoria exchanged the same vows, he felt that he could be content to die that very moment.

"I should like her mother to know as Victoria's married!" was his speech at the feast Mrs. Linnett gave in her little kitchen.

They went down the river to Greenwich; and surely never was there such a day! Old Euclid declared he had never known one like it. Bess and Roger thought it was no brighter, or warmer, or happier, than the one that had been spent on board the *Cleopatra* two summers before; but the other three were dead against them. Captain Upjohn maintained that there could be no question as to which day was the fairer one. Certainly no happier party ever strolled under the flitting shadows of the Spanish chestnut-trees in Greenwich Park, or ran down the slopes together; old Euclid himself running far in the rear with his shambling feet, and his grey hair blown about by the wind.

And the coming home again, up the river, in the cool of the evening, with the soft chill of the breeze playing on their faces! Euclid sat very still and silent, with Victoria and her husband on one hand, and Bess, hardly less dear to him, and Roger on the other. But his silence was the stillness and peacefulness of a happy old age, free now for evermore from all oppressive cares. To-morrow morning he would be up again at four o'clock, and go off to the market; but labour was no longer irksome to him. He was no longer drudging merely for a coffin and a grave. He was not now without hope and without God in the world.

They landed in the dusk, and brushed past an idler, who was lounging near the stage, watching the steamers come and go. But he started and stared as his eyes fell upon them, and with a stealthy step he dogged their way home. Not one of them looked back, no one suspected that they were followed, though he kept them in sight until he saw Mrs. Linnett watching for their return over the half-door of her little shop, and waving a white handkerchief to welcome them. Then he turned away, and sauntered homewards to the old place, where Euclid had saved, and hoarded, and lost the money which Roger had stolen.

"It's old Euclid!" he had muttered to himself, "and Victoria as grand as a lady; and little Bess; and who's the lad o' nineteen or so? Why! it must be Roger; my son Roger! And he's doing well, by his clothes! I'll be even wi' every one on 'em yet."

Chapter 20. BLACKETT'S REVENGE

It was five years since David Fell had first crossed the fatal threshold of the gaol. He had graduated in crime, and, being neither a blockhead nor a lout, he had developed skill enough to transgress the laws and yet evade the penalty. The untrained ability of an English artisan, and the shrewd tact of a London lad, had grown into the cunning and business-like adroitness of a confirmed criminal. The police knew him well by sight or report; but he had kept out of their hands for the last two years, in spite of much suspicion, and many hair-breadth escapes from conviction. He was doing credit to the brotherhood which had been forced upon him—the brotherhood of thieves. There was no disgrace for him now, except the disgrace of being found out.

In Prison and Out

Blackett had drifted back to his old quarters after Roger's time was up on board the *Cleopatra*, when he was no longer liable to be called upon to pay half-a-crown a week for his maintenance. David had gone with him; for there was a lingering faithfulness in his nature, which attached him to the only fellow-man who had not turned his back upon him when he came out of gaol. They had taken Euclid's old garret, which afforded good facilities for escape from a hot pursuit along the neighbouring roofs. For a little while David had felt mournful, or as Blackett called it mopish, at finding himself back again in the self-same spot where he had taken care of Bess, and helped his mother in her dire struggle for life. But presently the slight impression wore off. Blackett made much of him. They shared and fared alike; and lived together as though they were father and son.

It was a merry thought to Blackett that if the magistrates had filched Roger from him, they had thrust David into his hands, who was worth twice as much as Roger. He had spirit, and energy, and brains. The clear-headed sense of the honest carpenter, his father, muddled neither by drink nor ignorance, had descended to David in a measure that set him far above the poor, idle, terrified Roger, who had always cowered away from Blackett's savagery. He dared not be savage with David, and his respect for him almost amounted to affection. He was uneasy and anxious when David was long absent, and a welcome was always ready for him when he made his appearance in the garret.

Blackett said nothing to David of the discovery he had made of Euclid's dwelling-place, and the fact that Bess shared it. Carefully disguised, he haunted the taverns in the neighbourhood of Mrs. Linnett's shop, to pick up any information he could get concerning Euclid or his own son Roger. It was not long before some sailors, coming in from a long voyage, fell into the trap he laid for them, and talked of the heaps of money left with Mrs. Linnett, and the numerous sea-chests, filled with valuable goods, which she took care of for absent seamen.

Roger was gone to sea again, and Captain Upjohn had taken Victoria to visit his people at Portsmouth; so no one was left in the house but Bess and the two old people. It was a rare chance, if only he could get David to seize it. There would be Euclid's hoards into the bargain, for Blackett had never ceased to believe he was a miser, who had untold money secreted in holes and corners, if they could only make him reveal his hiding-places. But would David do it? There was an irresistible fascination to Blackett in the thought of at last fulfilling his threats, and wreaking his vengeance upon Euclid.

In Prison and Out

"Old Euclid!" he muttered contemptuously, "and Bess and a old woman! I could almost manage 'em myself."

He set craftily to work upon David's imagination, describing the sea–chests in the old woman's room, and their contents, as if he had seen them; and the hoards of the miser, who carried bank–notes stitched into the lining of his waistcoat, over which he wore a ragged old blouse. He dared not tell David the name of the miser, nor mention Bess. There was a soft spot still in David's heart, and Blackett knew it.

It had been a slack time of late, and all their ill–gotten gains were gone. There was no longer money to spend at the tavern, with its many attractions, at the corner of the street, and the garret was a miserable place to spend the whole day in. David was weary of having nothing to do, and there seemed no reason to him why he should not enter into Blackett's schemes.

It was a dark night when Blackett and David, having matured their well–laid plans, entered the quiet street, and surveyed the front of the house they were about to break into. The street lamps made it clear enough. On one side stood a high warehouse, empty and closed for the night, unless there should be some watchman in it, of whom there was no sign; on the other was an unoccupied dwelling–house, with the bills, "To let," grown yellow, in the windows. There was no light to be seen in any casement in the short street, for people who work hard go to bed early. To get to the little yard at the back of Mrs. Linnett's house it was necessary to turn down a narrow passage beyond the unoccupied tenement, and to climb over a wall in which there was no door. But there was no difficulty in doing this, even for Blackett, and David was over it in an instant. It was the dense darkness of a cloudy night, and the overshadowing gloom on the high walls surrounding them which created the only perplexity.

"It's as dark as the black hole," muttered David; immediately afterwards stumbling over a bucket, the iron–handle of which rattled loudly. He stood perfectly still and motionless, whilst Blackett grasped the top of the wall with both hands, ready for instant flight.

But there was not a sound to be heard in the house or in either of the buildings on each side. All about them there was a dead hush, unbroken by any of the numerous noises of life and toil with which the streets were full throughout the day. As David's eyes grew more accustomed to the obscurity, the dark sky became dimly visible overhead, cut by

In Prison and Out

the black outline of the surrounding roofs. This little, ancient dwelling-place, left standing between two more modern and much loftier dwellings, looked as if it was pinched in and hugged between them, with its old half-timber walls, and low, yet high-pitched roof, with a single gable, and a dormer window in it. He could make it out in the gloom, as he stood breathless and motionless in the shadow of the wall, listening for any sign of moving within. He was not afraid; there was nothing to be afraid of. In three minutes he and Blackett could be safe away. But he felt something like reluctance to break the stillness and tranquillity of the little, quiet house. Besides, there were only an old man and old woman in it. If they made any noise and resistance, what would Blackett do—Blackett, who was always savage when his blood was up? A number of thoughts seemed crowding through his brain, as he paused, with his eyes and ears all alert to catch any token of the waking and stirring of the old folks. But it was only for a few minutes. A church-clock near at hand chimed four quarters and then struck one. The spot was as desolate at this hour as it ever could be.

"We're not going to do 'em any hurt, you know," he whispered to Blackett, "for luck's sake. They are old folks, you said. We'll not hurt 'em."

"No, no," answered Blackett, laughing within himself, in the darkness. He would like to be even with old Euclid, and pay off the grudge he owed him these many years. There was bound to be a scuffle, though there was no danger for himself or David in it; two strong active men would find it mere play to overpower Euclid and Mrs. Linnett, and Bess would not count for much. What would David do if he found out that Bess was in it? If he could he would silence her first, before David knew who she was.

But though there was no light to be seen, and no movement to be heard in the dark little house before them, there was a quiet noiseless stirring within, which would have frightened them away, or hurried them on in the execution of their project if they had but known it. Mrs. Linnett was a light sleeper, and she had been broad awake when David stumbled over the bucket, and she heard the clatter as loudly as he did. Her bedroom was the one whose window overlooked the yard; and she had drawn aside the curtain a very little, and peeped cautiously into the gloom. Blackett's figure, with his hands upon the wall, ready to leap back from the inner side of it, was quite visible, even in the dark night. Would it be safe to increase the alarm of the thieves by showing herself? She was afraid to do that, lest it should fail. Her room was crowded with seamen's chests, piled one upon another, seven or eight of them, left in her keeping by old shipmates, who had trusted their possessions confidently to her care. She stepped quietly back to her bed, and woke up Bess, who was sleeping the deep unbroken sleep of girlhood.

"Hush, Bess, hush!" she whispered, laying a hand on her mouth, "there's robbers in the yard! Get up quietly and slip out at the front, lass, and run for your life to the police. It's for me and Euclid and the mates away at sea. It's nigh upon one o'clock in th' night; and we might all be murdered before anybody 'ud hear us shout for help."

So whilst David was listening and watching in the yard, Bess was rapidly getting on some clothing; and as Blackett began to remove the pane through which he could unfasten the kitchen-window, she was creeping down-stairs, from step to step, with stealthy and noiseless feet. She heard the quiet grating of the tool Blackett was using, and her teeth chattered with fright. But she stole by unseen into the little shop beyond; and letting down the old-fashioned wooden bar, and turning the key cautiously, she opened the door, closed it after her, and fled swiftly down the deserted street.

There was so little difficulty in opening the kitchen-window, that in a few minutes Blackett and David were both inside, and now lighted the small lantern they had brought with them. They moved about as quietly as they could, though they had no fear of the consequences of arousing the inmates, whom they could easily gag and bind if need be. But there was still no sign or sound of waking in the house. Mrs. Linnett, indeed, was standing within her room, with the door ajar, hearkening and peering down the staircase, and wondering, as she trembled with dread, how long Bess would be; but they could not know she was watching for them until they went up-stairs.

And now, fly, Bess, fly! If you meet any belated wayfarer in the street, or see the light of any watcher in a window, give the alarm quickly. Give way to no terror that might hinder you. Every minute is worth more than you can count. Run swiftly, for old Euclid, fast asleep after the day's toils; for Mrs. Linnett, shivering with helpless fright; for the mates at sea, and for Roger, whose goods are in danger. And yet, Bess, if you did but know who it is that has broken into your quiet house, as a thief and a robber, you would fly back more swiftly than you are running for help, and with your arms about his neck, as when you were little children together, and your voice pleading in his ear, you might save him even now, at the last moment!

In Prison and Out

Blackett cast a glance over the little shop, with its miscellaneous wares, and round the small kitchen; but it was plain there was no booty there. The miser's hoard and the seamen's chests must be in the bedrooms, and they wasted no more time before mounting the narrow and winding staircase. Euclid was not sleeping in his closet, as Victoria was away; and the door of the front room stood at the top of the crooked stairs. They pushed it open, and the light of their lantern fell full upon the old man's face.

"Why! it's old Euclid!" shouted David, in a loud and angry voice.

"Ay! ay! is it time to be stirring?" the old man asked, rousing himself and looking up in bewilderment.

"Curse you! you never told me who it was!" cried David, turning fiercely upon Blackett.

But Euclid had already sprung up, forgetful of his feebleness, and calling upon Mrs. Linnett to fasten herself in her room, he flung himself with desperate courage upon Blackett. Blackett shook him off with ease, and seizing him by the throat, threw him down on the floor, and knelt upon his chest, with a savage cruelty in his eyes.

"Get up!" cried David, struggling to pull him away, "you shan't murder him, and me stand by."

"I'll half murder him," muttered Blackett. "I'll have my revenge."

Then began a deadly conflict between them; Euclid, as soon as Blackett's hand was off his throat, helping in the fray, with the feeble daring of old age. The chair on which David had set down the lantern was upset, and the light went out, leaving them in utter darkness, as they swayed to and fro about the room, never loosing one another, amid oaths, and threats, and, smothered groans from Euclid, growing fainter and fainter, as Blackett and David fought above him.

But now Bess was speeding back again, with two policemen running at a few paces behind her. The clanking of their footsteps on the pavement below was the first sound which broke in upon the struggle, and brought it to a pause. David heard it first, and loosened his grasp of Blackett in an instant. The steps had not yet reached the door; and in a moment he was down the staircase, and ready for flight by the way he had come. But

In Prison and Out

Bess, whose light, swift feet had made no noise, was already within the house, and she sprang forward to arrest him, clasping him in her strong young arms, with a vehement and tenacious grasp, from which he could not free himself. The policemen were but a few paces behind her.

"Oh! be quick!" she called, "he's here. I can't hold him long."

Her voice was shrill and strained, but David knew it too well. It was Bess who was holding him with such passionate strength; and his own strength seemed to melt away at the sound of her cry. The little sister he had loved so well, and been so proud of. His poor mother's little lass!

"Bess," he groaned, "it's me, David!"

With a wild, terrified, heart–broken shriek the girl's arms fell from their close grasp of him, and she sank to the ground at his feet, as if he had struck her a deadly blow. But had he wished it there was no time to escape, for the foremost policeman caught him firmly by the arm, and held it as if it had been in a vice.

"If you want to hinder murder," cried David, "be sharp up–stairs. Take me along with you, but for God's sake, lose no time."

Were they in time? or was it already too late? Old Euclid lay motionless on the floor, his withered face and grey hair stained with blood; and Mrs. Linnett was kneeling beside him, calling to him to speak, or look up at her. The window was open, showing the way by which the murderer had escaped. The second policeman started off at once in pursuit of him; whilst the other, who dared not loose his hold of David, looked on at Mrs. Linnett's vain attempt to raise the old man, and lay him on his bed. The whole room was in disorder, for the short struggle had been very violent.

"I'm David Fell," said the prisoner, in a strange and lamentable voice. "I never knew as it was old Euclid we were goin' to rob. I'd ha' cut off my right hand first. Handcuff me, and tie my feet together, if you can. Only see if the old man's dead or not."

"Nay, I must see you safe first," the policeman answered; "none o' your tricks and dodges for me. Come along, and I'll send help as soon as I can."

Bess was crouching on the floor down-stairs, slowly coming to her senses; and David stood still for a moment, as the light of the policeman's lantern lit up her white and scared face and terrified eyes.

"She's my sister!" said David again, in the same strange and lamentable voice. "Bess, I'd have sooner drowned myself in the river than come here to spoil your life!"

Bess covered her face with her hands, shivering; and listened, in faint and deadly sickness, to the sound of David's retreating footsteps, till they were lost in the stillness of the night.

Chapter 21. WHO IS TO BLAME?

When Bess, after a few minutes of almost deadly anguish, crept feebly up-stairs, she found Mrs. Linnett still kneeling beside old Euclid, who was stretched upon the floor. The policeman's lamp, set upon the mantle-shelf, lit up his bloodstained face and hair, and displayed the disorder of the room. She helped Mrs. Linnett to lift up the old man and lay him on the bed, and then she sped away again to fetch a doctor, though not so swiftly as she ran before for help against the housebreakers. Would she ever run so fast again?

By the time she returned a woman had been sent from the police-station, and a policeman was on duty in the house. The doctor, who followed her quickly, after a brief examination of old Euclid, said he could discover no serious wound, but that it was impossible to tell how grave the injuries he had sustained might prove. He had the blood washed from his face and hair, and after that Euclid lay still, much as if he had been asleep; only his pulses beat very faintly, and life seemed to have ebbed away to its lowest tide.

The morning came, and policemen were coming and going all day long, examining the premises and asking the same questions over and over again—or so it seemed to Bess. Neighbours crowded in to chat with Mrs. Linnett about the perils of the night, and to take a peep at the unconscious old man, who had been almost, if not quite, murdered. The question was, whether he would die or live. David refused to give up his accomplice, but Blackett had been arrested on suspicion. Nothing more could be done until Euclid's consciousness returned, if it ever returned, and he could give his evidence. A policeman was stationed there until this should happen. At last night came on again, and Bess, refusing to leave old Euclid, persuaded Mrs. Linnett to go to bed; whilst the doctor, finding three or four neighbours whispering and buzzing in the room, ordered them all away, and told Bess to watch him by herself. She sat beside him hour after hour, sleepless, yet almost stupefied by her sorrow. Could it be true that David had done this cruel, wicked deed? And oh! if Euclid died, what would be done to him? The sickness of despair filled her whole heart as this thought came back to her, in spite of all her efforts to shut it out.

"Bess," whispered a very low, faint voice in the dead of the night, "it was our David!"

"Yes," she whispered back again in Euclid's ear. But a deep throb of agony struck through her as she heard him say it was David.

"He fought for me agen Blackett," said Euclid; "he saved my life. Blackett 'ud ha' murdered me."

With a loud sob Bess fell on her knees by the bedside. Thank God, David was not as bad as he had seemed! He had not joined with Blackett in his savage purpose. David was not a murderer!

Oh, what a load seemed suddenly rolled away from her girlish heart! Her brother was only a thief!

"He saved my life," murmured old Euclid over and over again, as though his brain was bewildered still. "Bess, he saved my life."

His faculties came back to him very slowly, and it was two or three days before he recovered the full possession of his memory, so as to be able to make a deposition before a magistrate. Blackett and David were committed to take their trial at the Central Criminal Court. Victoria had come back to help to nurse her father, and for a short time their life fell back into its old course, excepting that Euclid no longer started off for the market every morning.

But the dreaded day came at last, when Euclid and Mrs. Linnett, and poor Bess herself, were compelled to appear at the Sessions and give their evidence against David and

In Prison and Out

Blackett. Mr. Dudley had engaged counsel to defend David, that every fact in his favour might be made public, and his sentence, in consequence, be mitigated. There was not the shadow of a hope of an acquittal.

When Bess stood up in the witness-box she saw only two faces clearly. There was David, pale, abject, frightened, with bent head, and dim, mournful eyes fastened upon her; and there was the judge opposite to her, calm and grave, with a searching keenness in his gaze. As she told her name David's lips moved a little, as though he was repeating it to himself.

Unconsciously, merely answering the questions put to her, Bess told the story of David's two first convictions, and the sorrow they had wrought.

"He was always a good boy to mother and me," she said, sobbing, "and he's good to me still. He'd never be told where I lived for fear he'd spoil my life. Oh, Davy! Davy!"

She burst into tears, and stretched out her arms to him, as if she would throw them about his bowed-down head, and cling to him, in face of them all, in spite of his deep disgrace. David laid his head on the bar at which he stood, and shook with the sobs he forced himself to control.

He did not look up again until Euclid was taking the oath. The old man appeared many years older than he had done before the murderous attack made upon him. His grey hair was quite white, and his cheeks and temples had fallen in like those of a very aged man; but he smiled at David, and nodded affectionately. So far as the cruel assault upon himself went he completely cleared him; it was Blackett alone that had maltreated him.

"David Fell never lifted up his hand agen me, my lord and judge," said Euclid warmly and energetically. "He fought for me, and I'd ha' been a murdered man this minute but for him. Why I've known David ever since he was this high, and he'd ha' made a good man, if he'd had a chance. He hadn't a chance after he'd been sent to gaol, and his mother was as good a woman as ever you see."

At the mention of his mother David's face grew as pale as death, and his lips quivered. He fancied he could hear her voice calling his name. For years past he had tried to deaden the memory of her; but now it seemed as if he could see her plainly, sitting by the dim, red

In Prison and Out

light of a handful of embers, talking to him and Bess about their father. To work hard and honestly as his father had done had been his mother's religion, the simple code of duty she had tried to teach him. Thank God, his mother was in her grave, and knew nothing of his guilt and shame!

His brain grew weary, and he ceased to take notice of what was going on after Euclid disappeared. Different men stood up and spoke, some for a minute or two, others for longer, but he did not understand them; their speech was as a foreign tongue to him. His previous convictions had been very summary, and the proceedings now appeared complicated and perplexing. Why were they so long over this trial? Everybody knew he had broken into the house for the purpose of robbery. His first two trials, when he was a young lad, had not occupied five minutes each. Why were they so much more careful of him now when it was too late?

At last his wandering attention was caught by the utterance of his mother's name. He turned his eyes to the speaker, and never withdrew them from his face until he ceased to speak. It was the counsel whom Mr. Dudley had engaged for him.

"Elizabeth Fell was left a widow at the age of twenty–four, with a boy and a girl to provide for. What aid did we offer her? We told her she might take refuge in our workhouse, among the outcasts and profligates of her sex, where we would take from her her children, who were as dear to her as our children are to their mothers, and bring them up apart from her. If she refused such an offer we would leave her to fight her battle alone. She chose drudgery and hunger—a terrible disease, and death itself—rather than take our aid on our terms.

"When she lay dying, gnawed by famine, with a mere pittance of out–door relief, her son, a lad under fourteen years of age, ventured to go out and beg for his mother. He was ashamed to beg, willing, on the other hand, to work, having an ambition to tread in the steps of his father, the honest and skilful artisan. What did we do for Elizabeth Fell's child? We arrested him, dragged him before a hurried and overworked magistrate, omitted to investigate his statements, and after a brief trial of four or five minutes, sent him to gaol for three months.

"David Fell hastened home when his first imprisonment was ended, to find his mother still alive, but on her death–bed. In her dire extremity she had parted with the most sacred

In Prison and Out

treasure she possessed—her wedding-ring—and she and her young daughter had literally starved themselves to redeem this sacred symbol. It was redeemed the day after David Fell's release from gaol; but the ring given back by the pawnbroker was not the familiar, precious relic so perfectly known to them all. It had either been sweated by the dishonest pawnbroker or exchanged for another and a thinner ring. The lad, in a passion of mingled grief and resentment, rushes away to secure his mother's own wedding-ring. The man assailed his dying mother's good fame, and utterly reckless of all consequences, David Fell sprang upon him in a frenzy of hot resentment, and felled him to the ground. The pawnbroker was a householder and a ratepayer. Once again there was no investigation made, no credence was given to the boy's angry and bewildered statements. We committed him a second time to gaol for three months.

"These were the two first steps—two long stages—on the road to ruin, the road which has led him to this bar to-day. Who is to blame? The lad, willing to work, but untaught and awkward, with no training but that of the street, whom no man would hire for his want of skill and dexterity? Or the magistrate, overworked with a pressure of serious business? Or the police, with their legion of juvenile criminals, whose statements are mostly falsehoods? The magistrate cannot give the time, the police cannot give the trouble, to investigate cases like David Fell's.

"The boy was like other boys, our sons, with high spirits and heedless heads. Have we never known our sons beg, ay, and beg importunately for what they want? Do they not fight at times, on a tenth part of the provocation this boy had? I will go farther. Have none of them ever been guilty of some small theft? Would you send those thoughtless, passionate lads of yours, who are to come after you in life, as citizens standing in the places you win for them, would you send them for such crimes as David Fell committed, begging for his dying mother and defending her good name, to the black shadow of a gaol, and the deep brand of imprisonment? Would you bind your boys hand and foot, and cast them into a gulf, and if they crawled out of it, crush them down again because they brought with them the mire and clay of the pit? Yet this is what we do with our juvenile criminals.

"The prisoner is guilty of burglary. He is not yet nineteen years of age, and he has been already four times in gaol. I ask again, Whose fault is it?

In Prison and Out

"He must be punished? True. But let the penalty—too well deserved this time—be tempered with mercy. We have tried severity. We have confounded his sense of right and wrong; it is we who have extinguished the feeble glimmer of light his poor mother had kindled in his conscience. I ask you to remember the prisoner's sad career, his devotion to his mother, his love for his young sister, his defence of the old man from the murderous attack made upon him. I ask you to remember that, whilst he was yet a child, in this Christian land of ours, we sent him once and again to gaol as the fitting penalty for childish faults."

David heard no more, nor had he fully understood the words he had listened to. His throat was parched, and his sight was dim. The Court seemed filled with mist, which blurred all the faces around him. He stood at the bar for a very long time yet, before the policeman next to him nudged him roughly, and bade him attend to his lordship.

"Have you anything to say for yourself?" asked the judge.

"Nothing; only I'd ha' drownded myself before I'd ha' hurt little Bess or old Euclid," he stammered.

In a few minutes after he was led down a staircase into a room on the floor below the court, and a policeman was fitting him with handcuffs.

"What are they goin' to do with Blackett and me?" he asked.

"Didn't you hear the sentence?" rejoined the policeman.

"No," he answered; "I can't see nor hear nothin' plain."

"Ten years for Blackett" was the reply, "and two for you. You're let off pretty easy."

Chapter 22. THROUGH GAOL TO THE GRAVE

David returned to gaol, broken–hearted and weary of life. Circumstances had thrust him into a career to which he had not been born; he could not drift heedlessly with the tide that was rapidly sweeping him down to utter rascaldom. His early training and his faithful

In Prison and Out

love for his mother and sister set him at odds with the mass of young thieves, born and bred amid the lowest dregs of the London populace. There had always been a vital difference between him and them.

He had never ceased to be conscious of an aching sense of degradation and loss, lurking beneath the artificial pleasure Blackett had taught him to feel in the vicious habits of men like himself. He had learned to associate with them, but he had never been in heart one of them. And now that he had been blindly led into crime against the home that had sheltered Bess, and against her friend old Euclid, who had barely escaped with his life, he felt as if he had sunk to the last depth of infamy and wickedness.

It was little Bess herself who had hindered him from making his escape. Poor little Bess! how desperately she had clung to the thief, lest he should get clear off! Dreams of it visited him in his prison-cell. When he fell asleep he seemed to be about to make some hair-breadth escape into freedom and a better life; but at the last moment, when success appeared sure, Bess would snatch him back and plunge him again into his gulf of dark despair. It was always Bess who held him fast till his enemies, sometimes human, sometimes devilish, were upon him. And then, when he was recaptured, and she saw his face, who it was, and called him by his name, she would fall down at his feet and die; and it was his wickedness that had killed her! Such dreams as these terrified and scared him.

David became a loathing to himself. A thief! It was the name he had been taught to abhor and dread from his infancy. His mother's simple creed had been to be honest and industrious, and to take all that happened to her as being the will of God. But now he was himself the being his mother had most feared and hated. It was as if some tender-hearted man had found himself guilty of an act of savage cruelty; or an innocent, guileless girl had plunged unawares into an abyss of infamy. David had become the thing which he abhorred; he was an abomination to himself. Two years would soon pass away. But what after that? He would still be a thief when he was released from gaol, and the ranks of honest men would be more firmly closed against him than ever. If he could have his choice, he would stay within the shadow of the prison walls, and not creep forth again to find no comradeship except with thieves. His heart failed him to think of having no fellowship but with such men as Blackett. He knew that there was not a chance of anything better. The gaol-brand could never be got rid of in this life.

In Prison and Out

He was no longer classed among the juvenile criminals. He worked at his trade among the adult prisoners, but he held no manner of intercourse with any of them. The work he did was little, not enough to keep him from frequent punishment; but neither encouragement nor punishment aroused him to any interest in it. He was never heard to speak in answer to praise or blame. His eyes were often fixed on the floor, as if he was lost in a kind of dream. He was silent, apathetic, and sullen. Whatever was going on around him, he appeared deaf, and blind, and dumb. Often he looked almost imbecile.

Now and then a darker shadow brooded over his face. It was when the thought crossed his brain of how easily he could put an end to his misery, if he were but standing once more on the brink of the river. He could fancy he saw its rapid current hurrying away to the sea. Why had he never escaped from the wretchedness that hemmed him in by this swift and easy road? Here, in gaol, it would be difficult to make an end of himself. It had been done, but he shrank from the way to do it. If he could only fling himself into the cool, rapid river, and sink in it!

There was chapel for him, and daily prayers, and the chaplain's visits; but none of them brought comfort to his despair. They seemed to him but a part of the machinery of the criminal court and the gaol. The Gospel of Christ was presented to him in such a way as made it, to his bewildered and desolate soul, only a part of his punishment, as he sat in the gaol chapel, a criminal among criminals, with the eye of the governor upon him. If that religion was for any upon earth, it was for the rich and powerful, not for the poor and feeble like his mother, and the erring and sinful like himself! The poor were pinned down to suffering and crime, whilst the rich were fenced in from temptation to outward sins, and set in high places to make laws and enforce them. Such Christianity was no gospel to David Fell.

Day after day, night after night, through long weeks and months, did David's heart die within him. Very slowly, almost imperceptibly, his physical powers failed him also. His hand lost its cunning, and his sight grew dim. Wrapped up in his wretchedness he made no complaint, and asked for no favour. His body filled up its appointed place, sat at his bench, crawled to and fro along the corridors, crouched in his cell; but he hardly felt or knew what he was doing, or where he was. He was the mere shadow of a man; the life, and spirit, and heart of being was dying out of him.

In Prison and Out

There was only one thing that stirred the flickering life within him. There were the letters Bess wrote to him, always loving and cheerful, promising that all should yet be well for him when he was once more free. She would go with him to some far-off land, she wrote, and they would begin life afresh together. But David would shake his head mournfully over those dear promises. Would it not indeed spoil her life if he let her leave old Euclid, and Mrs. Linnett, and the home in which she was so happy? That could never be.

One Sunday morning, after chapel, he found a letter in his cell. He had been twelve months in gaol, and Bess had written three times. It was time for a fourth to come, and he seized it as eagerly as a man dying of thirst clutches at a draught of cold water. But this letter was not from Bess.

"Dear David,—I'm a seaman now, earning good wages, and I've saved twenty pounds; and Mr. Dudley says if I get on well in learning navigation I shall be a mate soon. So I've asked Bess if she'll be my wife. Oh, David! nobody knows how I love Bess; I'm thinking of her night and day when I'm aboard, and when I'm ashore I can't bear to be out of her sight. She's prettier and dearer every time I see her. But she says, 'No, I belong to Davy; he's got nobody and nothing save me.' She never says that she can't love me, or I'd never have wrote to you. Now I want you to write to her and tell her you'd like her to marry me, and you'll have a brother as well as a sister. It would be better for you if I married Bess instead of another man, because I couldn't never be ashamed of you, as Father's a thief, and my own two Brothers. If she married any one else, he might taunt her some day, and I couldn't. Don't stand in my way, dear old Davy. I'll be a good Husband to Bess, and a good Brother to you; and I'm earning good wages; and perhaps I may rise to be a captain, and then Bess shall be a Lady. Only write to her, and say you'd like to have me for a Brother, and you'll never repent it. From your loving friend,

"Roger Blackett."

David sat motionless for a long time, crushing the letter tightly in his feverish hand. There was no work to be done, and he had leisure to ponder over it bitterly. Roger Blackett! How well he could remember the timid, brow-beaten, half-starved lad, who lived in terror of his savage father. A poor, idling, weak, despised boy, held cheap by all the other boys in the street. The son of a notorious scoundrel, whose elder sons were London thieves. And now, after being trained on board ship, he was a seaman, earning good wages, and looking forward to be a mate, and thinking of marrying—ay, of marrying Bess! Some day he might rise to be the master of a vessel, and be called Captain Blackett, whilst he, David Fell, what was he?

A castaway, a housebreaker, and a convict!

Roger would marry little Bess. David seemed to see it in a dream; Bess in a house of her own, pretty, and loving, and good, with little children growing up about her, and Roger coming home from his voyages, bringing gifts from foreign places, to show how he had thought of each one of them whilst he was far away. A life of honest, cheerful toil lay before Roger, with gladsome home delights, such as make this earth a pleasant world to live in. He seemed to see the children's faces, and hear their voices ringing in his ears. All that for Roger; but what for him?

Death on a gaol–bed.

He felt it for a certainty as he crushed Roger's letter in his fingers. The passage through the gaol to the grave had not been a long one; and he was glad of it, if his dreary sense of making his escape out of an evil world could be called gladness. Death was very near at hand, and could not come too soon.

The next day his warder recommended him to go into the hospital, and he went. The medical officer could not say what ailed him, or under what name to catalogue his disease. There was no column in his report for hopelessness and heartsickness.

Chapter 23. OUT OF THE PRISON–HOUSE

Roger never received an answer to his letter to David. But a few days after it had been despatched, and after Roger was gone again to sea, there came an official permission to old Euclid and Bess to visit the prisoner. David Fell was dying, and requested to see them at once. There was no time to be lost if they wished to see him alive; and they hastened to obey the summons, scarcely realising the grief that had come upon them.

David had begged to be taken back into his own cell, where there was quiet and loneliness, rather than to lie dying in the midst of the rascality of a prison–hospital. A

In Prison and Out

softer mattress and pillow had been laid under him, but in every other respect the bare whitewashed cell remained as it was when he had entered it more than a year ago. Through the closely barred window, high up against the ceiling, could be seen only a patch of wintry sky, grey and cold with clouds. The heavy door, with its small round eyelet, through which the gaoler could at any time watch the prisoner unseen, closed quietly upon Euclid and Bess, as they entered David's cell, and stood just within it, as if afraid of stepping forward to the prison-bed.

He was lying with his eyelids fast closed, and his white and sunken face resting so still upon its pillow, that as they stood there hand in hand, hardly daring to stir, they believed that he was already dead. But when Bess tremblingly approached him, and laid her warm hand on the thin, skeleton fingers lying on the dark rug which covered him, he looked up at once into her face, with no light or smile in his eyes, but with a gaze of speechless love and sorrow.

"Davy!" she cried, sinking down on her knees, and laying her cheek close against his upon the pillow, "Davy! speak to me."

"Little Bess!" he said, "and Euclid!"

"Ay, David!" answered Euclid, looking down upon him in unutterable pity. The old man's face wore an air of peace and of quiet gladness, which had smoothed away its former gloom and roughness; and his voice fell more softly on David's ear than he had ever heard any voice, except his mother's and little Bess's. He turned his dim eyes to the old man's face.

"I'm dyin'," he said, "in gaol!"

Euclid only nodded silently, whilst Bess drew his chilly hands to her lips, and kissed it tenderly.

"It's been a cursed life for me," he groaned, "but it's almost over."

"Oh, Davy!" sobbed Bess, "if you get well, and only live to come out o' gaol, you and me 'll go away to some country a long way off, where you can live honest and happy."

In Prison and Out

"It's best as it is," he said, stroking her rosy face fondly with his thin hand, "I should ha' spoiled your life, little Bess. Roger 'ill make you a good husband, and care more for you when I'm gone; and you'll think of me sometimes. No, no. Hell can't be worse for me than this world's been."

"Davy! Davy!" she cried, "you don't think you're goin' there!"

"There's no other place for me," he answered; "folks don't go from gaol to heaven. I've broke God's laws; and they say He'll punish us worse there than they've punished us here. God couldn't set me free to go to heaven."

"But you're sorry," said Bess, weeping.

"Ah! I'm sorry I hadn't a better chance, like Roger," he muttered. "I might ha' made a good man; but it's too late now."

"God knows all about it," sobbed Bess.

"Ah! and God can forgive you yet," said Euclid. "Didn't Jesus forgive the thief that was dyin' side by side with Him when He was bein' crucified? A thief, David! Bess, my dear, you read it out to us, for fear I might make some mistake about it."

Still kneeling by the bedside, with David's cold hand clasped in her own, Bess read, in a faltering, sorrowful voice, these words:

"And there were also two others, malefactors, led with Him to be put to death.

"And when they were come to the place which is called Calvary, there they crucified Him, and the malefactors, one on the right hand, and the other on the left.

"Then said Jesus, Father, forgive them; for they know not what they do.

"And one of the malefactors which were hanged railed on Him, saying, If thou be Christ save Thyself and us.

In Prison and Out

"But the other answering rebuked him, saying, Dost not thou fear God, seeing thou art in the same condemnation?

"And we indeed justly; for we received the due reward of our deeds: but this Man hath done nothing amiss.

"And he said unto Jesus, Lord, remember me when thou comest into Thy kingdom.

"And Jesus said unto him, Verily I say unto thee, To-day shalt thou be with Me in Paradise."

"That's it," exclaimed Euclid, "the malefactors only received the due reward of their deeds; but He had done nothing amiss. They'd broke the laws, and were bein' crucified for it; but Jesus was bein' crucified with them! It seemed as if there wasn't any other place for them to fall into, save hell. But there was a road to Paradise even from the three crosses on Calvary; and Jesus was goin' up that shinin' road Himself. They might both have gone with Him to Paradise; and you can go to Him there from gaol, David. The poor thief was dyin', but it wasn't too late to ask Jesus to remember him. I don't say as you're fit to go to heaven, David; I can't say anything about that. But that poor fellow went into Paradise, with our Lord Jesus, Himself. That must be a place worth goin' to. He says 'In my Father's house there are many places,' and He'll know where you are fit for."

Euclid's face quivered and glowed with earnest entreaty; and his husky voice seemed to gain a softer and more appealing tone as he spoke. David fastened his hopeless eyes upon him, listening as one listens to the distant, far-off sound, which foretells that help is coming.

"Jesus Himself was bein' crucified as if He'd broke the laws as well as them," said Bess, a light shining through her eyes. "He hadn't ever done any sin, but it's like as if He said to Himself, 'There's poor wicked folks as will be put to death for their wickedness, and maybe they'll think I didn't come to seek for them, and save them as well as the rest, if I don't die like them.' He must have meant to save the worst folks, or He might have died different, not as if He'd been breaking the laws Himself. I never thought that of Him before. He came to save thieves and murderers; and so He died as if He'd been one of them. Davy! you're no farther away from Paradise than the poor thief was."

In Prison and Out

The faint dawn of hope in David's sunken eyes was growing brighter, as if the sound of help was coming nearer to him; and he grasped the hand of little Bess more firmly in his trembling fingers.

"Ay, there must be room for you there," said old Euclid. "He'll know where it's best for you to be. And oh! David! He loves you. Only think of that. Why! Bess and me, we'd have found a place for you, out o' love and pity, if you'd only lived to come out o' gaol; and His love's a hundred times more than ours. It stands to reason as His love is a hundred times more than what we poor creatures have. Only you think about Him, and call to Him. If you can't say nothing else, just say, 'Lord, remember me,' like that poor fellow on the cross beside Him. I wish I knew his name; but that don't matter. You'll not hear Jesus speakin' like he did, but all the same He'll say, 'To–day shalt thou be with Me in Paradise.' Bess, my dear, when we hear as David's gone, you and me 'll say, 'To–day he is with Jesus in Paradise.' It seems to me as if it 'ud be better than comin' out o' gaol into the streets o' London."

The tears were rolling down old Euclid's withered cheeks as David gazed up at him. The boy made a great effort to speak, but the words faltered on his tongue.

"A thousand times better, if it's true," he gasped.

"If it isn't true, there's nothing else for you or me of any good," answered Euclid; "we're worse off than dogs. If there isn't any God as loves us, nor any Saviour as died for us, this world's a cruel, cursed place."

"Oh, it's true!" cried Bess, clasping his hands fondly in her own. "I love you, Davy, and God loves you, and Jesus died on the cross with a thief beside Him. He wouldn't ever have done it, if He didn't love us all."

But the time allotted to them had expired, and the warder warned them that they must go in a few minutes. Bess laid her bonny face against David's dying head on the prison–pillow, and put her hand upon his clammy cheek. The last moments were flying fast. Yet what more could they say to one another? Would they ever see one another again? Was all the sorrowful past brought to this end at last? Must they leave each other here, and break for ever the bonds of love and memory which had linked their lives together?

In Prison and Out

One more minute only. Euclid laid his hand on David's chilly forehead.

"Good-bye; God bless you!" sobbed the old man.

"Good-bye," breathed David, faintly. "I didn't mean to be a thief. Good-bye, little Bess."

She pressed her lips to his once more in a long last kiss. Then they were compelled to leave him. The night was falling, and the light faded away slowly in the solitary cell. The warder came in to light the gas, but David asked to be left yet a little longer in the gathering dusk. The grey of the wintry sky glimmered palely amid the surrounding blackness as the gaol-walls vanished from his dim eyes, and it looked the only way of escape from the thick darkness of the bare cell. He was alone. Love had been forced to quit him before life did. There was no hand to hold his as long as the icy fingers could feel its loving grasp. No voice to whisper words of hope into the ear growing deaf to earthly sounds; no touch on the cold damp forehead, telling of faithful companionship down to the very threshold of death.

Now and then the warder glanced through the aperture in the thick door, seeing in the dim twilight shed through the prison-window that the prisoner lay still, and made no signs of needing help. Who among them could help him to die? The chaplain had visited him, and his friends had been to see him; there was nothing more to be done. The spirit, in all its ignorance and sorrow, bereft of human love, was slowly preparing to wing its flight into the dark and drear unknown. Alone and in prison David Fell was casting off the last link of the heavy chain of grief, and wrongs, and crimes which we bound about the boy when we sent him to gaol (for begging for his mother).

At last a nurse came in to see him. The heart still beat feebly, though the grey change that is the forerunner of death had passed over his face. She stooped down over him, for his lips moved, as though he were trying to speak into some listening ear.

"Lord, remember me," he whispered.

So God opened the prison-door, and set our prisoner free.

Postscript.—I earnestly entreat those readers who wish to know for themselves the facts upon which the foregoing story is founded, to read as diligently as they will find that I have done a book entitled, "The Gaol Cradle: Who Rocks It?" It is neither a bulky book nor a costly one. The gist of it may be gathered in two or three hours' reading; though it may well be pondered over, and if pondered over will haunt and trouble the reader's mind. It contains not only the problem of juvenile crime, but I believe in it may be found the solution of that problem.

No gaol for children. At least one country has come to this decision. In Germany no child under twelve years of age can suffer a penal sentence. Between twelve and eighteen years of age, youthful criminals are free to declare whether, while committing the offence, they were fully aware of their culpability against the laws of their country. In every case any term of imprisonment above one month is carried out, not in a gaol, but in an institution specially set apart, and adapted for young offenders. These institutions serve not only for the purpose of punishment, but also provide for the education of the wards; the neglect of education being recognized as one of the chief sources of crime.

"The Gaol Cradle: Who Rocks It?" You and I.

Printed in the United Kingdom
by Lightning Source UK Ltd.
102054UKS00001B/63